I0722192

Sky Court

Sky Court

FAITH MOSLEY

CIRCUIT BREAKER BOOKS

Circuit Breaker Books LLC
Portland, OR
www.circuitbreakerbooks.com

© 2022 by Faith Mosley

All rights reserved. No part of this publication may be reproduced or distributed in any form or by any means, or stored in a database or retrieval system, without the prior written permission of the publisher, except by reviewers, who may quote brief passages in reviews.

This is a work of fiction. Names, characters, businesses, places, events, locales, and incidents are either the products of the author's imagination or used in a fictitious manner. Any resemblance to actual persons, living or dead, or actual events is purely coincidental.

Book design by Vinnie Kinsella

ISBN: 978-1-953639-14-1
eISBN: 978-1-953639-15-8

Library of Congress Control Number: 2022942661

This book is dedicated to my brother,
Eric Brian Mosley
1965–2022

Part One

One

It was almost ten. The local radio station announced the big basketball game had ended. River City High was the winner, so I should have been celebrating with everybody else. Everybody else included the entire school and most of the town. Because this is a small town, people tend to get very excited about high school sports. I wasn't celebrating, though. I was wiping down counters in the Wise Owl, the café I work at after school. This was a Friday night, so we stay open until eleven. Most nights I have to be home by nine because the Wise Owl closes at eight, but my grandfather lets me stay out just past eleven on Fridays because these are work hours. Those are his rules, and since I live in his apartment, I abide by his rules. Even though he is eighty-three and I'm seventeen, we're a lot alike. We like plain clothes, KFC, and taking walks. We're both kind of quiet people, so rooming with him has worked out pretty well.

I wiped down the counters slowly while listening to music on the radio and imagining my future life as a tugboat captain on the Mississippi. I imagine quiet days and nights pulling barges or breaking up thick chunks of frozen ice so the river boat gamblers can keep partying into the night. I've never seen a Black woman tugboat captain before. I wonder if I'd be the first one. I daydream a lot because my current life is not great. It's not horrible, but it's not really too interesting.

I started to put the chairs on top of the tables when the door swung open and a red-cheeked man staggered into the café and sat at the counter. He was sweating, which was weird because it was probably thirty degrees outside. His sandy hair stood up in all directions. He slurred his words. I had to lean in close to hear him.

"Just coffee," he said. I poured him a cup of coffee and watched him closely. The phone was only ten feet from my hand, and I'm pretty fast. It's not that he looked dangerous, but he definitely looked troubled, wild, possibly drunk. I was more curious than scared. I'm a real watcher of people. I like to walk the streets of River City and take in all that life has to offer—faces, shoes, clothes, ways of talking, desperate stares, interactions between people, people and pets…everything.

This man looked around the café with eyes darting everywhere, like he might need a quick getaway. We were near closing, and my boss, Andy Hardwick, was out on a break. I decided to be kind. He looked like he could use the comfort. I offered him the last slice of pie. It was lemon meringue, and I don't like that kind of pie, so it was no problem offering it to this strange man. He accepted it and downed it in about four forkfuls. I refilled his coffee.

"Have you ever been in jail?" he asked. His plate was scraped clean, and he stared into my eyes.

"No," I said.

"Well, I may be going there," he said and sipped his coffee. His face relaxed after he said that, as if an enormous rock had been lifted off his chest. He started to cry and wiped his eyes with the sleeve of his ripped, down coat.

"What's wrong?" I asked. I felt scared but nosy too.

The man leaned over the counter. His eyes pleaded for me to understand. I could smell his breath. It had a whiskey smell to it even after coffee and pie. I know the smell. My grandfather drinks whiskey on Friday nights. He says it's a holdover from his working days when he'd celebrate weekends.

The man told me he'd been driving a box truck for work. He worked at some place in Galesburg, which is about sixty miles away. He'd been listening to the basketball game when he started out. About halfway to River City, we won, and he was excited and tired but wanted to celebrate because he went to River City High thirty years ago and even played basketball — which was almost hard to believe because he was pretty beefy. But he was also tall, so back then he'd probably been smaller. Anyway, he pulled over at a liquor store — The Pony Express — and bought a bottle of Wild Turkey. This was his way to celebrate. His eyes got big when he said this, and I refilled his coffee cup because I wanted to hear more from this strange man. He then said he sat in the cab of the truck and cranked the heat and just started tugging at the bottle trying to forget about his wife who had left him and taken his only friend on the planet, his seven-year-old daughter. He said he drank until it was hard to see, and then he started the truck back up and drove onto the road and just didn't care what happened. He said it was almost like he wanted an accident. He said the snow had started by then, just a light beautiful snowfall that reminded him of the first snow when he was a kid in River City, before girlfriends and marriage and a kid and his wife leaving him, before a mortgage he couldn't afford, before everything. He cried a bit as he unloaded all this on me, and I tried to follow it all. It was hard listening to this adult who had so much pain in one body.

I put on another pot of coffee and poured myself a bit because I didn't want to miss any of his words. The man said the snow picked up quickly. I know he was right about that because it was still snowing. And it was beautiful. Even from inside a tiny café, the snow was beautiful.

The man said he was getting closer to River City when, for some reason, he took the turn off to the peak, which is what locals call the collection of rolling hills that overlook the river. It's where kids park and make out. He said he just needed to see something or relive something — he didn't know which. The turnoffs were all wet and soggy with the snow, and he slowed down in his big truck to be able to make the tight turns. He said he wanted to go to a spot that was secluded, a spot that he and his wife used to go to and fool around. He said he should have slowed down, but didn't see the car in time and swiped it hard. He said the car slid down a hill, and he parked and ran through a curtain of snow to get to the driver's side. He yanked open the door and found two teenagers in the front seat, two young men with letterman jackets on. He said their pants were down. Both of them had their pants down. He shut the door gently and called 911. He said he just wanted to get outta there. He didn't want to have to explain any of this. It didn't make sense, anyway, and he didn't want to be connected to any of it. He'd given his name to the operator before he realized what he'd done, and that's when he jumped in his truck and drove here.

"You believe me, kid?"

I didn't know what to say. Luckily, I didn't have to say anything. Two police officers entered the café.

"Are you Larry Dale?" the tall, gray-haired one asked. I recognized him, and he nodded to me in an official way.

"Yes, sir," the man said.

"You reported an accident?"

"Yes, sir," Larry said. His face was red again, and his hair looked bad even though he'd smoothed it down a bit as he talked. He looked at me with big, scared eyes. I just looked back at him. I didn't know what to feel.

"Would you mind coming with us to the station? We need to get a statement."

"Yes, sir," he said. The three white men walked out of the café. "Thanks for the coffee," Larry called out as the door closed behind him. I waved.

Just then, Andy came back from his break.

"What was that all about, Casey?" he asked, leaning over the counter but still staring at the door.

"The guy with the police accidentally hit a car," I said.

"Oh. I was afraid he'd started trouble in the café."

"No. Everything here is fine."

"Okay. Why don't you knock off?"

"I haven't mopped the floor yet."

"Alberto can do it first thing. Go ahead on home."

I said okay and got my coat and backpack from the storeroom. Andy was a pretty good boss. He was forty-seven and had firm opinions and a full head of gray hair. He said he started going gray in his twenties, that going gray early ran in his family. I liked that he didn't seem to care. He'd often say, "These are the cards I was dealt."

On my way home, all I could think about was Larry Dale and his story, which was more like a confession. His eyes and his hair. So many pent-up feelings. He was about thirty years older than me and had been through a lot, practically a war. I wondered if I would look so wild and desperate at forty-seven. Would I even get to that age? I looked up at the sky and opened my mouth and tried to taste the new soft snow that was falling.

Two

I SAT ALONE AT A TABLE NEAR THE DOOR AND WATCHED THE popular kids laugh and talk, take pictures to post on social media, and throw food at each other. No one knew that the returning heroes of last Friday's game, Trevor Morrison and Steve Jones, both sporting fresh white casts soon to be covered in signatures, had been found in Steve's car with their pants at their ankles. Their car accident was big news, but there was no mention of how they were found. I knew because the man who hit them told me. I still wasn't sure what it all meant, but when the excitement died down for a moment, I noticed a look. It was a subtle look from Trevor to Steve. I don't know what it said, but it certainly said something.

Rowena Miller, who also sat alone, waved to me out of nowhere. I raised my hand at her and then turned to the window.

I eat alone because I don't really have friends at River City High. I had a fun hangout buddy in my sophomore year, but she moved to St. Louis with her family. Most of the kids at this school have known each other since kindergarten. That's small-town life. I didn't show up here until freshman year. Until that time, I lived in Chicago. A few years before I moved here, my mom left a note on the kitchen table and never returned. My dad didn't give me any explanation other than "Adults change and sometimes need to be on their own." He and I lived alone in a small apartment, but then my dad wanted to remarry, and his new girlfriend, Mirlayna, moved in. She wore a lot of makeup, fake eyelashes, and fluttery, sensual clothing. She didn't like me at all. I tried to be nice to her, but she always stared at my hair, which is a natural short afro. She hated that I only wore jeans and t-shirts or sweaters, and she sometimes made rude comments about my lack of fashion sense. My dad tried to help us like each other, but nothing worked, not even the trip to Disneyland. I'm not sure why this was his strategy since standing in lines all day under a hot sun surrounded by screaming kids is not exactly my idea of a good time. Mirlayna didn't enjoy the trip either. That was about the only thing we ever agreed on. After the trip to California, my dad helped me pack up my few clothes, some books, and my record player and then moved me down here to west central Illinois to live with my grandpa in a small apartment complex called Sky Court.

Living with my grandpa was an adjustment because he lives in another world where cell phones, TVs, and computers are evil. I had to learn how to live life without numbing out on TV. That was tough, and I miss it at times, especially when it rains. But having no TV got me outside. Walking the town became one of my favorite things to do.

My grandpa's name is Ernest Black, and he watched me a lot at first, but when he saw that I wanted a job and was committed to taking school seriously, he quit watching me. Now we're more like friendly roommates. He smokes a pipe and wears a lot of sweaters and loves fried chicken.

Both Steve Jones and Trevor Morrison also live in Sky Court. We say hi sometimes, but that's all. Just hi. Two letters. Then we look away. I'm not popular, and I'm not feminine, so I guess it would break some kind of rule for us to actually say more than two letters to each other. Sometimes I think Trevor wants to say more. We have physics together, and sometimes he lingers near my desk, but like I said, a rule could be being broken, so we keep to our own hemispheres.

The day after the return of the conquering heroes, everyone was acting normal—less high-fiving, more back to the books. Our final semester as seniors was just around the corner. Christmas was two weeks away. This was our last week of school before the holidays. I had tried to put Larry Dale's face out of my mind, but every night before bed, I'd just lay there wondering about him and his life and his daughter, his only friend. That's what he'd said. I wondered if he'd gone to jail or maybe lost his job. He was drunk driving.

I was daydreaming as usual, walking down the hall, barely paying attention to the shoulders I bumped into when a girl tapped me on my shoulder. She wore a plaid, wool skirt, leather calf-length boots, and a close-fitting sweater that made her look smart and different from the other girls in high school.

"Casey?" It was Rowena. She of the sudden, unexpected wave at lunch. Technically, she's a popular person and shouldn't be speaking to me, but since she spent spring semester in France on a Rotary scholarship, she's seemed different in class — quiet, thoughtful, and well, her clothes were stylish and quiet too. I noticed her when I first started school here because she was pretty but not stuck up, and she smiled at me once in the library when I was a sophomore. She was a cheerleader then.

"Yes?"

"I was wondering if I could borrow your notes from English last week. I was out with strep, and you seem like the only person who takes notes in there." She smiled, and the library moment from two years ago flooded my memory banks.

"Oh, uh, yeah." I gave her the notebook, a black spiral-bound one that I'd been very careful not to write anything personal in. I use my journal for that. She smiled again and said she'd get it back to me at the Wise Owl tomorrow night. I said okay and watched her walk away.

I walked home through the snow. My daydreams of Larry and his sad adult life had been replaced with Rowena's warm, brown eyes.

When I returned to the apartment complex, I stopped at the mailboxes in the courtyard to get our mail. That's when I spotted Steve Jones hanging around by the bike rack doing nothing. I stuck my key in our mail slot and rummaged around, but I watched him closely. Steve is tall, probably six-foot-three, and real skinny. He's what my grandpa once called a handsome, dark-skinned Black boy. He said this to me as a joke, to tease me because early on I guess he could tell I had no interest in boys, and he found this kind of humorous. Occasionally, just to rattle me, he'd inform me that a handsome, dark-skinned Black boy was my neighbor. Now we both laugh at that, but he'd really laugh now if he knew that that handsome boy might not be interested in girls either. Of course, I had no proof about that, but Larry's tale opened a door I'd never considered looking behind.

I got our mail and shut the slot door when I heard Trevor's laugh. It's an unmistakable high-pitched laugh. Then I saw the back of his shaggy brown head with no winter cap on. I watched them walk away together. Funny how you can know things about a person without knowing the person at all. I was tempted to follow them, but I had to get my own kitchen cleaned up before I went to work at the Wise Owl. We live on the second floor, and from the kitchen window I could see Trevor and Steve walking away from the complex heading out towards the little forest that begins at the back of the apartments. Steve limped with a waterproof cast protector snugged around his ankle. I guess he refused to use the crutches. I wondered if they were cutting through the woods to get to the mall or maybe hang out downtown or go to the movies. I wondered how it must feel to be popular but live a secret life. My grandpa came in just as I had finished doing the dishes.

"Casey Black," he said, "how was your day?" He sat the familiar red and white bag from Kentucky Fried Chicken down on the kitchen table and peeled off his coat and cap. He rubbed his shiny bald head. Maybe he used to do that when he had hair, and it was habit. For dinner on Tuesdays he always brought home fried chicken because of a two-for-Tuesday senior special, and he loves to take advantage of a senior special. He's eighty-three years old and always says, "I earned this." He set the newspaper down and started to set plates out for our chicken.

"I had a fall over by the chicken farm," he said. The chicken farm meant KFC.

"You're okay, though?"

"Yeah. I mean I made it home, but now my back and head are bruised, I think. Won't slow me down, but I have to be careful walking these wintry streets. Because when an old Black man falls, ain't nobody gonna pick him up."

I gave him a smile.

"It's true," he said. "The white folks will step over you, move around you, but they ain't gonna stop to help an old Black man, so I have to be extra careful. Remember that, little one." He loved to impart knowledge and life lessons. I listened to his words even though he grew up in a different era. I wanted to believe that white people would be kind to him, but his bruises told a different story, and he had walked on the earth for eighty-three years. Still, he liked life even though he knew people wouldn't go out of their way to help him. He had smile lines at the corners of his eyes.

I walked to work slowly thinking about life and how I might fit into this world. In Chicago, at the high school I would have attended, they had a gay-straight alliance. I would have joined that, but here there wasn't one. I never had a girlfriend or even knew how to get one, but I knew who I was. Who I was didn't belong here. This town is small and conservative. Very conservative is what my grandpa said to me one night, so I just have to bide my time. Those were his words. I don't say "bide my time."

The snow had started back up again, so the sky was white gray. It felt nice to enter the warmth of the café.

"Dishes are waiting for you, Casey." Andy greeted me and then went back to his conversation with a man at the counter who was crumbling crackers into a bowl of chili. I hung up my coat and put on my rubber apron and rubber gloves and started in on the stack of dishes. There's a daytime worker named Alberto, but by the looks of my stack of unwashed dishes and pots and pans, Alberto never showed up. I turned on the water to hot and began rinsing the dishes first before loading them into the tiny industrial dishwasher. I did six loads. I then filled the pots with hot water so they could soak. I immersed myself in this dishwashing process for over an hour. Around seven, I emerged from the kitchen and cut myself a slice of the dessert of the day, which was chocolate cake. I sat at the bar and ate while Andy schmoozed with the sole customer.

The snow was falling hard, and I sat there swiveled around, staring out the big window watching the ground become a huge white carpet. After the customer paid and left, Andy stepped out from behind the counter and said he'd be back in a few minutes. I said okay and continued to watch the snow. I felt mesmerized by its soft brightness. How could something so light and beautiful cause major traffic accidents?

I turned away and picked up the remaining plates and glasses and loaded them into the dishwasher. I went out front with a wet cloth to wipe down the counter, booths, and tables when I saw the article on the front page of a folded up *River City Current*. It read, *Local Child, Patricia Dale, 7, Missing*. That had to be Larry Dale's daughter. I knew it. I just felt it. Immediately, I could picture Larry, frantic, terrified with his thin hair sticking out in all directions. Poor Larry.

The article said that Patricia had last been seen at school waiting for her mom. The mom, Katrina Lassiter Dale, had been questioned but claimed to know nothing. The article said that though the parents are separated, "they are united in their quest to bring Patricia home." Wow, I thought. Life is intense.

I finished the countertops and swept the floor, which was dark with slush. I put chairs up and mopped. I placed yellow cones out to prevent anyone, mainly Andy, from marking up my floor, and then I sat down in the kitchen and re-read the article. There was a number if anyone wanted to help. I dialed the number from the old phone on the kitchen wall. I guess Andy was a bit like my grandpa who hates cell phones. I was surprised when a man answered.

"Hi, is this Larry Dale?"

"No. This is his brother, Daryl. Who's this?"

"My name's Casey. I met Larry the other day in the Wise Owl Café. I work here. I was calling to see if I could help." There was a pause for a moment. I heard people in the background.

"Yes. Thank you for calling. You can help. You could post flyers for us. Could you do that?"

"Yeah. Sure."

"Okay. We'll have flyers for pickup at Leman's Grocery in the morning. You can get some there."

"Okay. Is Larry doing all right?" Another pause.

"Not really. He's losing it." We hung up then. I could just imagine Larry losing it. His hair and red face. I left work that night a little after eight and started to walk home the usual way on Bridge Road, but for some reason decided to take the wooded path.

The sky was bright with snow even though it was nighttime. I trudged through the snow leaving first footprints. When I was deep into the woods, I stopped by a tall pine tree, a natural Christmas tree, and took off my gloves. I took some snow from a branch and tasted it. It was fresh and cold. I smiled and put my gloves back on.

I hurried on because I had homework to do. Before crossing a small footbridge that rose gently above a stream that was still flowing, I stopped. I froze, as people say. I froze because I saw Trevor and Steve in a lovers' embrace. They were kissing passionately. I looked away. I then looked one last time and ran back from the direction I came from.

"Must have been a busy night at the Owl," my grandpa called out from our tiny living room. I was out of breath from the run and tore off my coat and hat. In my room I stripped myself naked and ran down the hall to the bathroom. Once in the shower, I let the hot water stream down my body. Afterward, I sat alone in my room on the bed wrapped in a long beach towel. I couldn't stop replaying the image in my head of Trevor and Steve. It made me think about my own loneliness. That night I noticed a pit in my stomach.

Three

The big game had been a triumph for River City, who hadn't claimed the Countywide Championship Tournament for thirty years. The plan after the victory that night was for everybody to meet up at the peak. This included the whole team, the cheerleaders, girlfriends of players, and close associates. Trevor and Steve went early. They showered in the locker room and went straight to the peak, beyond the usual meeting spot. They drove until they found their place, a little turnout that was mostly hidden unless you knew where you were going. They'd parked and embraced. Things moved fast, and soon their pants were down around their ankles. That's when Steve cried out. A box truck slammed into his Ford Focus. Trevor didn't have time to react. The little car, a gift from Steve's mom for being a basketball phenom, for getting good grades, and for not doing drugs, took the hit and flew over the hill and rolled once.

"You're lucky," Steve's mother said as she stared down at her son in the hospital bed. He tried to sit up, but his head hurt. He rubbed his short afro. "You and Trevor were both lucky. Someone called in the accident. You're blessed you only broke your ankle." Martha patted her son's cast and smiled.

"Can I go home now?" Steve asked. Martha looked at the chart and then at her watch.

"The doctor will probably release you in a few minutes," she said. Martha had worked as a certified nursing assistant for twelve years. She knew all the routines and hospital protocol even though she was one of the lowest paid hospital staff. She'd wanted to become a nurse but something—generally time or money—always stood in her way. Steve was her pride. She wanted for him what she never had for herself, so she sacrificed. He'd already received two scholarship offers. It was up to him now to make a decision. This ankle injury was not going to slow his velocity.

"Martha, can I have a word." Dorothy, a nurse on the floor, smiled at Martha. Martha squeezed Steve's hand and walked out into the corridor.

"Hi, D," she said.

Dorothy moved close to Martha and in a lowered voice asked how Steve was doing.

"He's gonna be fine. What's up?" Martha waited.

"Look, it's not my business and probably means nothing, but the EMT told me the boys were found with their pants down," Dorothy said. Martha frowned. Dorothy looked concerned, and Martha stepped back.

"I'm not sure what you're implying, Dorothy."

"I'm not trying to start rumors, but I thought you should know is all," she said and turned away.

Martha stood for a moment alone in the corridor while a

voice came on over the loudspeaker paging a doctor. An orderly pushed a gurney past her, and the elevator doors opened and closed. Martha blinked and returned to her son's room.

Dr. Mathers released Steve with crutches and a boot to protect the cast. He'd congratulated him too with a hard slap on the back and a big toothy grin. On the drive home, Martha studied her son's profile.

"Why do you look so worried? You survived," she said.

"I can't remember much," he said.

"Well, the doctor said that your short-term memory might return in a few days. Trauma does that, you know?"

"Yeah." Steve reached down and touched his ankle cast and then looked out the window. The snow was falling gently, and he felt anxious about everything. As they pulled into their assigned parking space at Sky Court, Steve's phone rang out the *Mission Impossible* theme song — Trevor's ringtone. Steve didn't answer. Instead, he sent a text message and hobbled out of the car. It was dark and slick outside.

"Let's get you to bed. You can talk to friends tomorrow." Steve obeyed his mother's gentle prodding and followed her into the apartment. He was tired after the big win and then an accident. But before the accident? What had happened? What had he been doing with Trevor? He could guess, but how were they found? Did anyone know? Steve crawled into his twin bed and set a pillow beneath his injured ankle as he'd been instructed to do. He laid back with his hands behind his head after saying goodnight to his mother and wondered if anyone knew anything. His phone rang out the catchy theme song again. He answered.

"You okay?" Trevor's voice was raspy and tired sounding.

"Yeah. I'm in bed, man. You okay?"

"I've got a cast on my wrist, and my dad's been yelling at me, but what else is new?"

"What happened before the accident, Trev?"

"We were fooling around, dude, then a friggin' truck barreled into us."

Steve closed his eyes. "But how were we found? Were we clothed?"

There was silence for a minute, and then Steve could hear Trevor's dad's baritone voice yelling at him to go to sleep, then Trevor was back.

"Sorry. My dad's happy we won but pissed about the accident. He thinks I'll lose my scholarship to that piddly community college."

"Hey, a free ride is a free ride," Steve said.

"Easy for you to say, Mr. University of Illinois." They laughed, forgetting the accident for a moment. "I miss you, Steve."

"Shut up, man."

They hung up, and both boys laid awake for some time before falling to sleep.

When Monday rolled around the kids at school treated the boys like heroes. Steve put his fears away when no one mentioned the actual circumstances around the accident. The heroes survived, and everyone was happy. Casts were signed and photographed for Snapchat and Instagram. Steve and Trevor laughed and smiled and kidded around. No secrets were revealed. But Steve's fears came back when Connor Cole, the police chief's son, entered the cafeteria. He was tall and blond and looked like a basketball player, but he wasn't good enough to be a starter. He was always on the bench. He came in and sat at the end of the table. He smiled for a moment but didn't laugh and didn't attempt to join in the fun. Trevor looked at Steve then. Their eyes met, and they wondered if he knew. When Trevor looked up, Rowena was waving at them. They waved back and smiled.

Trevor didn't know what to think about Rowena. He'd never really thought about another person's feelings until he and Steve had confessed their attraction to one another. That had been a year ago, and they hadn't talked about it much since then, but whenever they had the opportunity to be together privately, they would take advantage of their time. Trevor thought about Steve's feelings in relation to himself and about his own feelings, which were torn and twisted like an old bedsheet. Looking at Rowena, he wondered if she knew about his feelings for Steve.

Rowena sat at a table near the popular table but not at the popular table like she used to. She was fine eating on her own, and her friends knew it. She had become a quieter person since her spring semester abroad. During her intensive immersion into a new culture and language, her parents had gotten a divorce. Her father stayed in the family house, a three-bedroom ranch-style house in a solid middle-class neighborhood. Rowena and her mother had moved to Sky Court Apartments because Rowena's mother said she needed a fresh start without constant reminders of her old marriage. Since her parents' divorce and her time in France, Rowena had quit cheerleading and started smoking. She told Trevor that she just felt quieter now and couldn't be a cheerleader anymore.

Rowena waved to Casey. Casey reminded her of a neighbor girl in France that she'd had a crush on, not a quick crush either, but a labored, sweat-inducing crush that she'd never really been able to shake. She'd seen Casey at the apartment complex but had never stopped to talk. Rowena had never described herself as shy, but she definitely felt a bit nervous when she saw Casey in English class. Casey waved back and sat alone at a table near the window and stared outside. Rowena texted a message off to Carly: *You'd never guess who I'm staring at :).* Carly was her best friend and Steve's girlfriend. Carly quickly fired back: *Ooh, can't wait to learn more.*

Carly had missed the big game and the accident because she had been out of town attending her grandfather's funeral. Rowena kept her in the loop. Carly and Rowena had been friends since elementary school. In fact, Carly lived just two houses away from Rowena's dad. After Rowena moved, Carly said she didn't mind going to see Rowena at Sky Court. She went there anyway to spend time with Steve. Rowena, Carly, Steve, and Trevor often found themselves together due to proximity and convenience.

Connor rose slowly and tossed his sack lunch into the garbage can. Trevor scooted away from Steve when Connor approached. "You guys missed a great party at the Peak. Too bad you were busy celebrating on your own," he said. Steve and Trevor said nothing.

They both watched Connor leave the cafeteria. He looked over his shoulder at them before walking through the double doors. Trevor turned to Steve with big eyes.

"Chill out. He don't know nuthin.'"

Four

I DON'T KNOW WHY I WENT TO LEMAN'S GROCERY THAT MORN-ing and picked up flyers. I guess I wanted to help Larry Dale find his missing daughter, but to be honest, there was more to it than that. I think I wanted to understand how a popular high school basketball player grows into a big, thin-haired, sad man with wild eyes. Why did he get married in the first place? How did the kid happen if he wasn't happy with his life or with his wife? Why drink whiskey and then drive a big truck? We all know the statistics! I had so many questions about his life story that I felt like I had to get closer to the main character. Also, I had an English assignment that was due before Christmas break. The assignment asked us to do a character sketch of someone we do not know very well. We were tasked with observing a person, any human being, and writing about them so that if someone else read our description, she could clearly see this person in her own head. And to be fully honest, thinking about Larry was a distraction from thinking about Trevor and Steve in their romantic embrace and why seeing them together made me feel so lonely.

I mean I have fantasized about being with a woman, but I've never had the opportunity. I'm only seventeen, and I work and have school. When would I find a girlfriend? Where? How? But Steve and Trevor found each other. How did that happen? When my mind drifts back to the other night, I stop my brain and refocus on the search for Larry Dale's missing child, Patricia, age seven. Now I have the flyer to help keep me on track.

At lunch time, I clung to my stack of flyers as if they were some kind of life preserver. When I looked up, I saw Rowena Miller smiling at me. She waved again, so I waved back and then turned to stare out at the snow. Maybe people in Europe are friendlier than in America, and she learned new ways to relate to people while she was abroad. Or maybe she wanted to be a friend?

I couldn't just keep the flyers. The point of getting them was to expand the search, get exposure for the missing Patricia Dale, so I mustered up the courage and stood up. I started handing out flyers to kids at lunch. Kids took them and looked at me waiting for my explanation of why I was handing them out. It was almost as if they'd all been programmed with the exact same response, looking at me with an open, questioning mouth like a baby bird waiting for food. When I handed one to Connor Cole, he took it, studied it, and then stared at me with a nervous face. I thought I saw his lip twitch.

"Good luck with this," he said. He folded up the flyer and stuck it in his biology textbook before getting up and walking away. I'd always thought Connor was an odd kid, but his dad is the chief of police, and he probably knew something about the case that nobody else knew, so maybe he was just being discreet. I don't know. I continued to hand out flyers to the baby birds, and then I stuck some on the main school info board, which is mostly stuff for sale or trade (mostly video games) and club meet up times. I watched the clock in the hallway. I needed the school day to be over. I just wanted to be alone. This place felt like a pressure cooker sometimes.

When school let out, I didn't go home. I walked to the town square because the grocery store lady told me that there was a rally at three thirty, and that Larry Dale would be there to encourage the searchers. My plan was to see Larry and then go directly to work. I walked through the snow and was thankful that it was so light. I almost laughed. For some reason snow can put me in a really good mood.

The rally had already started when I reached the courthouse steps. There were about fifty people standing around. Some had cups of coffee in their hands. I saw Larry, who was in the same down coat he wore the other night at the café. His hair was more pressed down, but his cheeks were bright red, and his eyes were bulged out with either desperation or fear of public speaking. He stood in front of the microphone to address the crowd, but the sound didn't work. A large white woman, almost as big as Larry, in a long women's down coat, walked up and switched on the microphone. Then Larry started to speak.

"I want my daughter back," he said. The crowd went silent. "I need my daughter back," he said. The snow landed on his coat and on his head, and then tears started rolling down his cheeks. The people holding coffee cups stopped sipping their coffee and just stared at Larry as he began sobbing. The big woman in the long down coat stood next to him for a moment and then took him by the arm and led him away, and then a man who resembled Larry came to the mic and thanked the crowd for coming and for their support and directed people to grab flyers and join the arranged search groups. I figured he must be the brother I spoke to on the phone, Daryl. He seemed to have all the information. It's probably nice to have an older brother covering all the details. Being an only child, I wouldn't know.

I decided to join the search. The groups were color coded. I joined the green group because the assigned search area wasn't too far from Sky Court, and I knew my grandfather would have something to say about me participating in white folks' business. That's what he would call it. Maybe he was right, but I felt like I knew Larry, and I wanted to help. I didn't really have to tell my grandfather about the search, but we rarely keep secrets from each other.

We were given a special police number to call if we found clothing or anything connected to Patricia. If we found her body, which a deputy from the Sheriff's Department said in a hushed voice, we were not to touch anything. We were to call for backup and secure the area by staying there and directing any pedestrians away from the crime scene. I really enjoyed feeling like I was part of an official operation.

I was given a map of the green search area, and I studied it. I didn't know any other green team members as they were all older community members, so I just studied my map.

When I looked up, I saw a tall, blond figure. It was Connor Cole. I wondered if he was on the green team. Maybe his dad made him come out and participate. I could imagine that being a police chief's son would be tough. He turned and walked away from the group. He slunk away like he didn't care. His hands were shoved in his coat pockets, and he didn't appear to have a map or any flyers.

I looked at my watch. Shoot. I was going to be late for work.

"You're late, Casey." Andy was pouring coffee for a man at the counter.

"Sorry, boss. I was at the rally for the missing girl."

"They're not gonna find her, or if they do, she's dead already." Andy put the coffee pot down and walked back to the kitchen to flip a burger.

"Why would you say that?" I hung my coat up and reached for my rubber apron.

"Because it's true. Too much time has passed. Her dad probably killed her in a drunken rage and can't even remember doing it," he said. I watched Andy prepare a hamburger, add French fries and garnish to the plate, and head for the swinging door.

"I think you're wrong," I said. "She's alive, and I'm gonna help find her."

"Good luck with that, but don't be late for work," he said. I started rinsing a pile of plates and loading the dishwasher.

Five

Just before eight at night, Rowena walked into the café. I watched her as she looked at the other diners and sat at a booth near the window. She then watched as Andy put on his coat to leave. "I'll be back later," he called out to me as he left the café. I waved at him without asking where he was going. I was pretty sure I already knew the answer.

Rowena looked back at me and smiled as she put my black spiral notebook on the table in front of her. I walked over to her.

"Hi."

"Hi," Rowena said and slid the notebook over to me. I smiled at her. "Thanks for the notes. Those were good."

"Oh, anytime. Do you want to order anything?"

"I should probably go."

"Cup of coffee?"

"Um, okay," she said. I hurried back to the counter to grab the pot and poured her a coffee and then set cream next to the cup.

"Sugar's against the wall," I said.

"Thanks," Rowena said. "You live in 17B." Her big brown eyes stared up into my face.

"Yeah. I do."

"I live in 10B with my mom. Just me and my mom. My parents got divorced," she said and reached for the cream.

"Oh. I live with my grandfather. My mom disappeared, and my dad remarried."

"Oh." Rowena smiled. I smiled back and then walked away to refill a customer's coffee.

When the last paying customer walked out the door, darkness had settled over River City. The snow had continued, but it was now just a light dusting like powdered sugar shaken from a bag. Rowena's third cup of coffee was half full, and I had finished mopping the kitchen floor. I put away the mop and emptied the wheeled bucket full of water.

Andy walked through the door. He barely had any snow on him, so I knew he hadn't gone far, which told me he was out seeing a woman who lived above the drugstore across the street. He never said anything about it, but I saw a woman's silhouette in the window a year ago and put the pieces together after the third or fourth time he took an extended trip to the drugstore. I enjoyed the quiet hours without him there. I could easily serve up coffee, cake, and make a cheeseburger or club sandwich. Andy nodded to me, and I nodded back. Rowena stood up, and Andy looked at me.

"She already paid," I said.

"Okay," he said. "I'll close up. Have a good night."

Rowena followed me out into the night. We didn't speak at first, just walked. I felt my stomach get tight from nerves. We walked over snow-covered sidewalks until the sidewalk ended and we neared Bridge Road. It was Rowena who suggested we cut through the forest. I remembered what had happened the last time I took the shortcut. I wondered if the two lovers would be at it again.

"I only take this shortcut if I have company," Rowena said, "because my mom's terrified that I'll get snatched."

"Why would you get snatched?"

"Because I'm a seventeen-year-old girl. That's why. And crazy men like to snatch young girls and torture us." Rowena laughed. She had a soft laugh that bubbled up at the end. It made me smile. "Aren't you afraid of being snatched?"

"I never thought about it," I said. "I have too many other things to think about."

"Like what?"

"I have a job, school, my grandfather to think about, and now this." I showed Rowena one of the flyers I was passing out earlier. Most of the flyer was a picture of seven-year-old Patricia Dale. Rowena studied it with the light from her cell phone. I studied Rowena's hand and face and short, curly, dark brown hair. Her big, brown eyes were protected by long eyelashes that caught the falling snow. Rowena handed the flyer back to me.

Just then, a large deer moved through the forest. Rowena grabbed me and screamed. I instinctively wrapped my arms around her. Then the deer jumped and tore through the woods.

I could feel Rowena's warm, coffee-scented breath on my cheek. I then felt her warm lips touch mine. They were so soft, and then they were gone. Rowena laughed, and we walked further into the woods without speaking. Just before the clearing and the path to Sky Court, Rowena stopped.

"Thanks again for your notes. They were really helpful."

I wanted to say something, but then Rowena's cell phone rang.

"Oh, it's Carly. I gotta go." She went to the left, and I walked to the right. We lived in the same building, but we each walked to the entrance closest to our unit.

The apartment smelled like sweet pipe smoke, so I knew my grandfather was sitting out on the balcony. We have two chairs out there with a narrow table in between them. I could see his bald head from the living room. He should have had a hat on. I picked up his navy wool cap and opened the sliding glass door.

"Grandpa, here." I handed him the hat.

"Thank you, baby. How was the job?"

"It was good."

"Sit down, here," he said. "What's this all about?" He held up a flyer. I must have left some on the table. His face was staring straight ahead into the whiteness of the sky. He held his lit pipe in the other hand. Its embers were a dark orange, and the rich smell drifting from his ancient pipe made me feel sleepy.

"I'm handing those out and posting them."

"Why?"

"I know the father of the little missing girl. His name's Larry."

"Why would you know this Larry?"

"He came to the café one night and unloaded a heavy story on me. The police came because he was drunk driving, and his older brother said he was basically coming undone."

"Okay. None of what you are saying sounds good to me. You need to stay out of this white folks' business. They get all caught up in strange dramas that do not involve you or me. You need to steer clear of this mess."

"But I want to help find his kid. I mean, regardless of her race, she's missing and needs to be found."

"Drunk driving. Police. Uh uh, I don't like this one bit, but you are your own person," he said and turned his eyes back to the night sky.

I got up and went to the kitchen. I made a cup of chamomile tea. I could still smell my grandpa's pipe smoke. He smoked most nights, and I noticed when he had some prophetic statement for me, he was smoking his pipe. I wouldn't call him psychic, but he definitely felt things in a very special way.

I sat on my bed for a long time before taking a shower and climbing under the covers. When I finally did lie down, all I could think about was Rowena Miller's soft lips on mine. Rowena's kiss was so light, so brief, I wondered if it had really happened. Thank you, deer, for scaring her into my arms. I wish I would have kissed her back or caressed her hair or neck. Instead, I just stood there in a state of shock.

Before I fell into a deep sleep, I wondered why I had never considered the possibility of being snatched by a crazy man and being tortured. I prayed that this fate had not befallen Patricia Dale.

Six

Trevor Morrison lived with his dad, Dean, and older brother, Jay, who worked at a lumber yard. His dad rarely worked because he received a disability check from the Department of Veterans Affairs to compensate for a back injury he received in the military. Trevor dreamt of leaving home next year and starting his own life at college. He'd often fantasized that he and Steve could have their own apartment and get a dog together, but he knew this wasn't going to happen because Steve was going to the University of Illinois and he was going to a community college with a mediocre basketball team. He daydreamed about it all the time, though, because it helped get him through his days, which could be tough. His dad drank too much, and then he'd get mad and start yelling, and then might get into a fight with Jay. If Jay wasn't around, he'd pick on Trevor.

Trevor stared out the window at the snow and held his left arm, the one with the cast.

"Good thing it was your left wrist and not your right one," his father said, "or you might have to kiss that mini-scholarship away."

"Yeah, I was lucky."

"Damn right you were. We should sue that piece of shit driver who lost his kid."

"It wasn't that big of a deal, Dad."

"Don't tell me what is and what isn't a big deal. You think you'd be eating those eggs and bacon for breakfast if I had that attitude? I had to practically kick down the door to the VA to get them to deal with my claim. Those bastards didn't want to give me the rating I deserved, but I appealed that shit and got one hundred percent total. Okay. Total!" Trevor had heard it all before. He just wanted to get to college and forget about his home. "You gotta fight for what's yours, kid."

Trevor finished his breakfast. He didn't feel like eating, but he knew his dad would lay into him if he didn't clean his plate. Jay walked in the front door as Trevor was washing his plate. Trevor knew what was coming. He tensed his shoulders and clenched his teeth.

"Where the hell have you been?" Dean stood up and headed for the living room.

"I'm too tired to deal with you right now," Jay said as he fell onto the torn couch. Dean hovered over Jay and stared hard at his eldest son. Jay wasn't as tall as Trevor and Dean. He was five-nine and had thick blond hair. Trevor was tall and had brown hair like Dean. From the pictures he'd seen, Trevor knew that Jay took after their dead mom, Linda. She was small and blond. Sometimes it seemed to Trevor that his dad just stared at Jay as a memory of his deceased wife drifted by.

"You need to pay your part of the rent today," Dean said.

"Okay. I'll get you the money this afternoon," he said. Jay worked full-time and always had money. He'd even given Trevor movie money in the past.

"You need to get your own place soon," Dean said and then sat down in his recliner.

"Why's that?"

"'Cause I'm tired of seeing your face. Your twenty-two years old. Time for baby bird to leave the nest." Jay got up and walked down the hall.

Trevor went to his room, packed his backpack with his textbooks he hadn't opened the night before, and walked back down the hall.

"Hey, Trev?" Jay said as Trevor passed his bedroom.

Jay was sprawled on his twin bed with his door open.

"Yeah," Trevor leaned into the doorway.

"How's your wrist?"

"Mending."

"Mending? You sound like Dad."

Trevor smiled and walked on. He called "later" over his shoulder to Dean and closed the apartment door. He walked straight to Steve's door, but there was no answer. They had been walking to school together since Carly had left town for her grandfather's funeral. Trevor called Steve on his cell phone and waited. It went straight to voice mail. This wasn't like Steve at all, so Trevor took off alone and walked fast in the quiet early morning. The sky was white, but the snow hadn't started falling yet. On his way out of Sky Court, he saw Casey and waved to her. She waved back as he walked on.

When he reached the student parking lot at River City High, he saw Carly's old black VW Bug. She was back, so she must be with Steve. Trevor kicked at a snowbank. It wasn't that he didn't like Carly. He did. It was that now he would have to take the backseat to her. That's how it had been all year. She got priority, even though he knew Steve loved him more. He knew it.

He could feel his anger rising, and he stopped walking and took several deep breaths. His brother had taught him this breathing technique to calm down to prevent fighting. Jay had gotten into a lot of fights over the years, even though he wasn't a big guy. Eventually, he decided to teach himself how to get calm to put a stop to stupid behavior. Trevor leaned against the wall of the building that held the swimming pool. He took in several deep breaths and extended his arms out to his sides, opening his chest wide. Deep breaths. He did six of these and then walked to the school entrance.

He could see the back of Carly's head. She was at Steve's locker, and Steve was pulling books out. They were laughing, and Carly was talking fast. Carly, who is Chinese, stands one solid foot shorter than Steve. Trevor always thought that she and Steve made a funny-looking couple. Trevor didn't want to stop and talk. His stomach heaved when Steve made eye contact with him. Carly suddenly threw her arms around Trevor, and then he heard Steve's laugh and couldn't maintain his separateness. The three of them walked down the hallway with Steve using his crutches and Carly carrying his books.

Seven

I have to admit that I was a bit scared to go to school the next day. I wasn't sure what I was going to say to Rowena when we met up in English class. I got through the first half of the day okay, and lunch was fine because I didn't see her. She walked into English class about a minute after the bell and sat down in her seat, which is one row over and one seat behind mine. She touched my arm when she walked past, and I just stared straight ahead at Mr. Belner.

We were reading *The Grapes of Wrath*, and the conversation went pretty good. I contributed to the discussion, and Mr. Belner did a lot of nodding when I spoke. He thanked me for my comment, and then he gave us the next assignment early, which was more reading and an essay on a time when we felt displaced. We still had the character sketch to write. I feel anxious when I have multiple assignments, but Mr. Belner did this often, he said, to prepare us for college.

The bell rang, and I gathered my stuff together. Rowena walked up to Mr. Belner to say something, and I left the classroom. A couple of minutes later, Rowena was beside me pushing open the doors and stepping out into the winter glare of the sun on snow.

"I missed a couple of hours because my dad tried to break into our apartment after I left for school," she said. "My mom called me in tears just before class started, so I ran home. The police came, and it was a whole scene." We slogged through a foot of snow on the ground.

"Is your mom okay?"

"I guess so. She went to her therapist's office after dropping me off. I just wish she hadn't even called me. There was nothing I could do," she said.

Rowena turned to walk home. Sometimes I go home before work to decompress from school, but I didn't want to walk any further with Rowena, so I left her to go straight to the café. As she walked away, I noticed how her curly hair looked so soft. I wondered what she thought of our intimate moment the night before. Because of that one brief kiss, she had become super special to me, but she didn't feel like a girlfriend yet, just a friend with a mom in crisis.

When I walked into the Wise Owl, Andy waved me over.

"Casey."

"Yeah?"

"That guy Larry dropped these off for you," he said and handed me a stack of flyers. "And he said to say thanks."

I took the flyers from Andy. "How'd he look?"

"Larry?"

"Yeah."

"He looked very shaky, on the brink of a breakdown. I'd steer clear of him."

"I'm helping with the search."

"That kid is dead. I'm sure of it," Andy said and then walked away.

I put on my rubber apron and started rinsing the dishes and loading them into the dishwasher. On about my third load, the front door opened and I heard boisterous laughter. When I looked out into the dining area, I saw Steve and Trevor seated at a booth with Rowena and Carly. Andy took their orders and then cooked up several hamburgers and batches of French fries. He looked over at me and rolled his eyes as if to say, "Aren't high schoolers a drag?"

Rowena saw me and waved, and I waved back.

"Do you know them?" Andy asked.

"We're in school together," I told him. He shook his head. I knew that he'd been bullied in high school. Thirty years later, he still has a hatred for the entire high school community. He prefers his patrons to be from River City College or the local older folks.

It was hard not to think of Rowena due to her physical proximity, but I stayed the course and washed load after load of dishes. After I'd finished every last dish, I focused on scrubbing the pots I'd let soak, and then I swept the floor. When I looked out at the dining area and saw that they were still eating and laughing, I took a hot pail of water into the bathroom and scrubbed down the floor and then did the sink and toilet. When I was putting away my cleaning supplies, Andy looked at me. His thick gray hair framed his concerned face. In that moment he looked like a teacher or a parent.

"What's eating you?" he asked.

"Nothing. I'm doing my job," I said. Andy just nodded and watched me work. By the time the four friends rose to leave, I didn't have any other tasks to lose myself in. I wiped the counter down, and then Rowena waved goodbye. Carly smiled. The guys just walked out the door. Andy cut me a piece of the chocolate vinegar cake he knew I loved and then poured me a coffee.

"Take a breather," he said. I watched him grab his coat off the hook and head out across the street. I knew he was off to a romantic rendezvous or whatever. I ate my cake and sipped the coffee I'd grown accustomed to since starting at the Wise Owl. I studied the flyer that Larry had left for me. Patricia wore a red sweatshirt and had a big smile. She had a blond ponytail and shiny blue eyes. Who would snatch a child? And why this one?

Since the café was empty, I decided to pull out my notebook and jot down some ideas for my paper on feeling displaced. I wrote about the first thing that came to me when I closed my eyes and concentrated on the word *displaced*. I remember my dad telling me that he needed to start over in a healthy relationship, and that his new girlfriend also needed a fresh start. He'd taken me to my favorite pizza place. I was chowing down on a large slice of cheese pizza when he hit me with "so you'll be staying with my dad down state." We'd just returned from the fateful Disneyland trip, and I knew I hadn't scored any points with his lady, but I was his flesh and blood. I figured I was higher up on the food chain, but I'd been wrong. I'd been naïve. That was a word that Mr. Belner used a lot. "Don't be naïve," he says in class. Well, I was naïve to think that my dad was going to pick me over this new *healthy relationship*. When I packed my bags and boarded the Illinois Zephyr to River City, I felt displaced. I liked my grandfather well enough, and I was lucky that he loved me enough to take me on when my dad remarried, but I never thought we'd be roommates. I mean, I thought I'd have two parents. When my mom disappeared, I thought, *Well, I still have the one dad*, but when I sat down in my train seat with my duffel bag, I realized I just had me.

Eight

Rowena, Carly, Steve, and Trevor huddled next to Sky Court's storage unit. The sky was clear, but the night air was freezing. Rowena still enjoyed the group hang outs, but she had someone else on her mind. She tried to make eye contact with Carly, who had pressed herself into Steve's down coat and was continually giggling at his incomprehensible mumbling of a song he didn't really know the words to.

Trevor stood next to Steve too and inhaled his friend's cologne. It made his head dizzy, and he wanted to kiss Steve, but he knew nothing like that was going to happen for a long time and certainly not in public. Rowena smiled at Trevor, and Trevor smiled back. Steve screamed out when Carly tickled him, and that made Trevor laugh. He reached out to tickle Steve, too, and Carly laughed at his attempt, but Steve knocked his hands away.

"Cut it out," Steve said.

Trevor laughed and continued to try and tickle his friend. Carly tried to hold Steve still, but Steve became angry and yelled at both of them to stop. The fun moment disintegrated into an awkward silence, and then Rowena told a story about a boy she went to school with in France who was not ticklish at all, so everyone tried to tickle him. He loved all the attention, all the hands on him all the time. Everyone pretended to listen, but Carly's eyes were confused. Trevor looked to be on the verge of tears.

Just then, Casey walked by with her big backpack stuffed with books. Rowena tried to wave at her, but she didn't seem to notice them. Rowena couldn't tell if Casey really hadn't spotted them or if she was just pretending she didn't. When Casey put her key in the gate door, Steve said, "She's a lesbian." Carly giggled. Rowena noticed Casey pause. She had no doubt heard Steve. Instead of responding, she continued on as if she hadn't heard anything. She went upstairs to her apartment. Rowena picked up her sleek book bag and said she had homework.

"Wait, don't go in yet," Carly whined.

"I have a paper to write," she said and then smiled at her friends. They all said goodbye, and Carly gave her a big hug. When Rowena walked up the stairs, she stopped in front of Casey's apartment, but then kept walking down to her door.

Rowena entered her apartment and smelled her mom's cooking. Her mother, Barbara, was seated in the living room with her eyes closed, a glass of wine on the coffee table in front of her, and headphones covering both ears. Rowena dropped her book bag and picked up the album on the end table. Chopin. Classical stuff she was not into. She put the album down and watched her mother's eyes open slowly. Barbara smiled at her daughter.

"There's some veggie soup on the stove and bread in the oven."

"Thanks." Rowena walked to the little apartment stove and lifted the lid on the pot. It smelled good. She ladled soup into a bowl and sat down at the table.

"How was school?"

"It was okay. Boring mostly."

"Anything new happen?"

"Nope."

"Make any new friends?"

"That's a weird question for the end of a semester, mom."

"Sorry, honey. Just trying to make an inroad." Her mother smiled at her. She was used to Rowena's slightly anti-social behavior these days. She wasn't sure if the change had happened after the France semester or the divorce, or if it was just typical teenage behavior. Sometimes, though, she did miss the former bubbly cheerleader.

"How was therapy?"

"It was a big help. I'm sorry I dragged you into the whole mess. I just needed some support," Barbara said.

"What happened with Dad?"

"I think your father now understands what a restraining order means." Rowena didn't press any further. The trouble between her parents was their problem, not hers. She just wanted to finish high school and go to college. She'd applied to the University of Illinois and Middlebury College because of their language programs. She wanted to return to France and live there for three to five years. Maybe be a journalist abroad. She wasn't sure yet.

When her mother closed her eyes again and immersed herself in music, Rowena finished her soup and went to her room to think about being displaced. That was easy for her. Her childhood home was three miles away in a nice neighborhood where nothing was subsidized. People had cars and nobody rode the bus. She almost started to cry but stopped herself. She picked up her phone and punched in the phone number she'd found written with a Sharpie inside the cover of the notebook Casey had loaned her. She had written it down before giving her back the notebook, just in case.

Nine

Sweet-smelling pipe smoke filled the apartment. The room was cold. I could see my grandfather's bald head above his chair back on the balcony. The sliding door was open, so the cold air had found a home inside 17B. "Lesbian." Steve's word stayed with me but didn't pierce me. He only made me consider who I already knew myself to be. Takes one to know one. He had Trevor, and I had nobody, really. Just one kiss to remember and hold on to. One tiny memory. I dropped my backpack on the floor and headed out to say hello.

"Hey, Grandpa." I walked out to the railing so he wouldn't have to stretch his old man neck.

"Hey, young one. How was work?" He coughed, and the pipe shook in his hand.

"I stayed busy all night," I said.

"That's important," he said and then focused in on me. "It's good to earn your own money, Casey, but don't push it too hard. You gotta enjoy your youth," he said and winked at me through watery eyes. The phone rang inside the apartment, and I walked away to answer it. I dragged the phone cord into my room when I heard Rowena's voice.

"Hi," she said.

"Hi," I said.

"I just wanted to apologize for what happened outside," she said. "I know you heard what Steve said about you." I could hear her swallow.

"I know Steve meant to insult me, but I am a lesbian. I'm not insulted," I said. A silence followed, and then Rowena laughed. I smiled.

"What do you think about Steve?" I asked.

"Steve's a jerk," Rowena said.

"Is he?"

"Well, he could be nicer to Carly, so yeah, I think he's a jerk. I mean Trevor is his best friend, and I don't think he's that nice to Trevor either, so he's a jerk." There was a pause, and I listened to her breathe, and then I took a chance. This was out of the box for me, but I felt gutsy in the moment.

"What do you think about me?" I heard an inhale and a pause and then an exhale. Maybe she was smoking.

"I think you're sweet."

Ten

I COULDN'T SLEEP THAT NIGHT. I MEAN ROWENA USED TO BE a cheerleader, and here she was calling me at home and talking to me as if we were friends. She didn't mention our kiss, but that's okay. She thinks I'm sweet. I tossed and turned all night. In the morning, I made breakfast and then found my grandfather in his bed sipping coffee. He usually gets up before me.

"Why are you being lazy?"

"I am not lazy, kiddo. I'm tired. See how you feel when you're eighty-three years old. And this has not been an easy eight decades, let me tell you. There have been some primitive roads I've walked. Okay. Definitely not a cakewalk," he said and sipped more coffee.

"Do you want any toast or eggs?"

"No thank you. I'll just sip my cowboy coffee." He smiled and rubbed his bald head. I'll never understand how he can drink boiling water over coffee grounds. No milk or sugar.

I walked to school the long way because I wanted to savor the feeling from the other night. I don't know if Rowena felt it, but I definitely felt something. Maybe romance. Maybe just understanding. I still had the kiss at the front of my brain. Maybe I should have asked her to walk to school with me.

I was thinking a lot of Rowena thoughts when I spotted the police cruiser up ahead. The snow had started up again, but it wasn't heavy, and I could see Connor Cole step out of the car and shut the door. He didn't wave to his father. He stomped off, and then I saw Officer Cole get outside the car and yell something to Connor, but it was muffled in the snowfall. I could see that he was upset.

I rushed up to the cruiser, and Officer Cole turned towards me with his serious face.

"Hi, Chief," I said.

"Hi."

"Um, I was at the rally the other day." He just stared at me. "The one for Patricia Dale."

"Oh, yes."

"Any leads?"

"Uh, we're doing all that we can at this point. We're still conducting searches, and we're questioning the family, of course, but it's not … we'll keep everyone posted," he said. I could tell I'd caught him at a bad time, but I still wanted to help.

"How's Larry?"

"He's struggling. Do you know him well?" His thick gray eyebrows came together then, and I realized he was an old man to have a kid in high school.

"No, not well."

"Well, I see you've got flyers."

"Yes."

"Well, keep flyering, and we'll do another neighborhood search tonight. Can you help?

"Sure. When I get off work," I said.

"Great. And what's your name?"

"Casey, Chief. Casey Black." He nodded and then stepped back in his car.

I got to school a little late, and when I walked in the double doors, I walked right past Steve and Trevor. I looked Steve directly in the eyes, but he didn't say anything. He just adjusted his crutches. Trevor carried his books. There was no sign of Carly.

Eleven

That night at dinner, Steve sat quietly while his mother talked about her day at the hospital.

"I just wish I would have completed my nursing degree when I was younger. It's such a hustle with work and adult life," she said.

"Well, Martha, life is full of disappointments," Steve said.

"I'm Mom to you, mister," she said and smiled. Steve smiled back. "I've noticed over the years, Steven, that you do that when you really want to talk."

"Do what?"

"Call me by my first name," she said. "What's wrong? You afraid your injury will jeopardize your scholarship?"

"No. Coach already said I'd heal fine and be good. I'm okay," he said.

"I don't believe you. You know there was a time when you'd tell me everything. You'd tell me so much stuff. I wish it was still like that." Steven studied his mother then. She was only forty-two and had been on her own since his father walked out on them when he was three. She never dated after the divorce. She must be lonely.

"Mom?"

"What?"

"Are you lonely for a boyfriend?"

Martha laughed out loud and had to put her fork down.

"No, Steven. Sometimes … once in a while, but mostly I don't need the headache."

He nodded as if he understood.

"If I wasn't around you coulda gotten married again," he said.

"You had nothing to do with me not getting remarried. Did you not just hear me say I don't need the headache?" Martha finished her baked chicken and peas and took her plate to the sink.

"So you're not tired of being alone?"

"No. I'm tired of being broke. Steven, you're deflecting," she said and sat back down to look at her almost grown son.

"What does that mean?"

"You're avoiding talking about yourself."

"There's not that much to say about me. I'm just trying to survive high school."

"Survive it? I thought you enjoyed it." Steve shoved his plate away and sat still. His eyes filled with tears, and Martha reached across the table to touch his hand. He let her make contact for a moment and then pulled away. "Steven?"

"I have homework, Mom." Steve stood up and hopped over to the couch, where he found his backpack. He started in on homework at the coffee table. Martha watched him wipe away silent tears and then left him to go do the dishes.

When Martha had finished the dishes, she went back over to Steve and joined him on the couch. She put her hand on his shoulder. She had not mentioned the circumstances connected to the accident that Dorothy had relayed to her at the hospital, and the fact that he and Trevor had their jeans at their ankles did not necessarily mean anything, but she wished Steve would open up to her. When she jokingly poked him in a rib, he did not respond. He made marks in his notebook and ignored her presence with a sudden deep interest in his homework.

"I love you, Steven. No matter what," she said. The clock in the kitchen ticked away.

Twelve

By the time I finished work and joined the search party,
it was already going on nine in the evening. It was close to my
Friday Night curfew of eleven o'clock. I'd have to watch the time.
I found a small group of people crunching through the snow.
They moved in a line, and they moved slowly like soldiers walking
through a field of land mines. I didn't really want to join the group
and walk so slowly, so I was relieved when I saw Larry Dale step
out of his brother's truck and approach the tented area where
there was hot coffee and cider, more flyers, and another group
of people asking Chief Cole a lot of questions. Larry didn't speak
to the chief. He got coffee and stood alone by a large juniper
bush. His hair was still a mess, but he smiled when I waved and
walked over.

"Hey, you're the kid from the Wise Owl," he said and extended
his hand.

"Yeah. Casey," I said. We shook hands. Neither of us was wearing gloves, so our hands felt cold to the touch. "How are you
doing?"

"I'm not doing too good. I'm losing hope, and I feel totally powerless." Larry started to cry big tears, his shoulders shook, and I had no idea how to offer comfort. "Hang in there," was all I could think of to say. I waved my green-colored band in front of him to show him I was part of the search. "I better go join the group," I said.

He tried to smile at me through his broken, tear-stained face. I hurried into the woods, and I searched on my own, walking as slowly as I could while staring down into a vast white carpet.

Around ten thirty at night, I was about to wrap up my own search and get home. I still had homework to do, and I was beat. I was somewhere near my own apartment complex but still about a half mile away when I heard rustling in the bushes. I saw Steve leaning back as if he was stargazing. He was leaning against a rotten log, and there was Trevor with his head in Steve's lap. Steve gently stroked Trevor's hair. They were talking quietly. I felt guilty spying on them, even if it was accidental. I ducked down behind a bush to camouflage myself, and that's when I spotted Connor Cole. He was watching them from behind a tree, and he had his phone out. He was filming them. I backed away from my bush and kept backing up careful to stay low, but then I stopped. Goose bumps crawled up my arms. I could not let this happen, even if Steve was a jerk to me, so I did something totally out of character. I took a deep breath and then ran with all my might and plowed into Connor Cole.

"What the!" Connor yelled, and I felt the hardness of his long lean body beneath his winter coat. He flipped backward, and I rolled off him. Suddenly Trevor was behind me with bright red cheeks, and Steve's handsome face a wall of silent shock. Connor got up slowly. He grabbed his backpack, which had fallen off his shoulder, and took off at top speed. Steve made no attempt to follow him with his damaged ankle, and Trevor was so shocked he just stood there staring at me. His thick eyelashes blinking in the moonlight.

"I was part of the search team for the missing kid," was all I said. Trevor and Steve stared at me. "I was heading home when I saw Connor spying on you."

"Thanks," Steve finally said and slowly hobbled to where their backpacks lay. Trevor followed, and they moved stiffly into the darkness of the forest.

When I could no longer hear their muffled voices, I started walking home. I noticed something glowing in the snow. I bent down and uncovered the phone that had recorded the moment. Connor's phone. He must have dropped it when I tackled him. I stuffed it in my pack.

When I got home, I found my grandfather asleep in his bed with his little room heater turned on high. I turned it off and unplugged it to prevent a fire. My grandfather's breathing was jagged and labored. I watched his old body rise and fall. His pipe sat on the nightstand next to his bed. His house shoes were neatly lined up in front of the bed. His watch and an old ashtray sat on the dresser in front of a couple of family photos. I left his door open and turned up the heat in the apartment.

I think I was in shock. Now Trevor and Steve knew that I knew about them. I felt scared. I still had goose bumps. Finally, I made a cup of tea and called Rowena. I wanted to spill the whole story, but I couldn't get much out. I felt nervous when I heard her sleepy voice come on the phone.

"I'm sorry to wake you, but I needed to talk..."

"Casey?"

"Yeah."

"Hey, it's okay. I was thinking about you. Did you finish your character sketch for English?"

"Not yet. I decided to tackle the displacement paper first," I said.

"Me too. This is hard, and I really have a lot to say about feeling displaced."

"Me too."

"Really?" The conversation helped calm me down. I stayed up for an hour and talked with Rowena, and then I finished my paper. I didn't go to sleep until about three in the morning. I did not tell her what I saw.

Thirteen

When Trevor gently closed the door to his apartment, the living room light flicked on, and his dad was seated on the couch holding a can of beer surrounded by several empties. The smell of rancid food hit his nostrils hard, and he wanted to go back out into the cold. He stopped and waved slowly to his father, who put his beer down.

"It's late. Way past curfew!"

"What curfew?"

"The one I just started, mister! Your ass needs to be home before eleven at night every night!" Dean slurred his words and pumped his drunken fists. Trevor watched his dad attempt to stand up, stumble, relent, and then collapse back onto the couch.

Trevor noticed that the picture behind his father was badly slanted, as if it had been knocked out of place. He walked up to his father and stood close enough to touch him. He reached behind him and straightened the picture. It was a landscape painting, and in the corner it read, *Linda*. Trevor could almost remember sitting beside his mother in a pile of leaves on a warm fall day in the countryside. Was it a memory or a daydream? She had her easel and painting supplies, and he was just happy to be with her as the sun shined through dazzlingly bright leaves dangling from the branches that seemed to embrace them.

Dean watched Trevor step back and then walk away. He felt his anger seep from his body and puddle somewhere out of reach. Trevor's eyes were sad but bright in that moment, and Dean looked away. When he heard Trevor close his bedroom door, he bent over with his head practically on his knees and sobbed for everything he had lost.

Trevor woke the next morning to shouts coming from the kitchen. It was Saturday, and he had planned to go to the movies with Steve. The sound of his father's angry voice seemed to grow like a funnel cloud moving closer and closer, growing louder and louder until he heard heavy footsteps moving down the hallway. He closed his eyes and tried Jay's breathing technique to relax his muscles. He heard the slamming and opening of a door, more raised voices, and finally, Jay very clearly saying, "I'll be out in twenty-four hours!" That was the end of the argument, and the apartment grew quiet.

When Trevor heard the front door close, he climbed out of bed and walked to Jay's room. His brother had stuffed a duffel bag with clothes and was packing all of his muscle car magazines into a shoebox. When he saw Trevor standing in the doorway in his underwear, he nodded to him. Trevor walked into the room and sat on the bed.

"Where are you gonna go?"

"I'm gonna crash at Diane's if she's cool with it," he said and then ran his hand through his thick blond hair.

"Why do you have to move out today?"

"Because our father's an asshole." Jay grabbed a black plastic bag used for leaves or yard waste and started chucking his boots and sneakers into the bag. "I'm sick of his shit. He's always on me for something, and I pay my share of the rent." Trevor looked at the room that seemed smaller than his and suddenly felt very alone. He didn't spend a lot of time with Jay, but he counted on seeing him daily, and now things would be different. He didn't like the feeling of aloneness that suddenly enveloped him.

"Can we still hang out?"

"We barely hang out now," Jay said as he walked out of the room with a large sack in tow. From the living room window, Trevor watched his older brother toss his belongings into the back of an old, beat up Toyota Celica. When the car left the main road out of the complex, Trevor turned and stared at the landscape painting on the wall and cried.

Fourteen

My grandpa surprised me by waking up before me and making pancakes for breakfast. He hadn't done this in a long time, so I was surprised when he knocked on my door and told me to come and eat. He even brewed coffee in his old Mr. Coffee instead of his usual scalding water over grounds.

"Now, look, Casey, I have to go to the hospital this afternoon for some tests," he said. The Mr. Coffee made brewing sounds and gurgled.

"What kind of tests?"

"Lung tests of some sort. Don't worry about me. I'm okay," he said and then ate his food slowly. I watched him eat. He stopped to cough and then stood up and walked to the sink where he dropped off his plate. He turned and smiled at me as I ate. "You're almost grown," he said and rubbed my head as he walked out the door. The old Mercury Montego pulled out of our assigned parking spot, and Grandpa waved to me before driving down the just-ploughed street. I waved back and then washed the dishes.

I still had the cell phone from last night, but I had no idea what to do with it. I couldn't bring myself to watch what Connor had captured on video. It just felt like a huge invasion of privacy. So instead of obsessing over the phone, I poured myself a mug of coffee, sat down on the couch, and started writing a character sketch of Larry Dale.

I wrote about his hair and his sad eyes and broken face, about how he confessed the night of the big game and how, even though he caused an accident, he seemed like a victim because of his tortured conscience and his wrecked marriage, but mostly because his only friend was his young daughter who was now missing, which made me think of him as a loner type like myself. I was wrapping up the paper when there was a knock at the door. We rarely have visitors, so I jumped when the knock came.

I looked through the peephole. It was Steve. He was leaning awkwardly against the door because he didn't have his crutches. I opened the door.

"Hey," he said.

"Hey," I said. Steve stared at me and waited.

"What's up?" I replied.

"Can I come in?"

"Okay," I said. I stood back and let Steve hobble into the living room. He stood by the couch and looked around our place. I didn't know anything about Steve other than he was a good basketball player, he lived with his mom, and he dated Carly Lee but was really in love with Trevor Morrison. At least it looked that way. The morning was gray and cold. The lamp gave off an aura of warmth, and Steve finally sat down where I'd been sitting. He probably thought our home was sparse and maybe sad. I had no idea what a stranger would think of our place. My dad had come to visit me once, but he just shook his head and laughed at our old rotary phone and 1960's radio that still worked just fine. My grandpa was kind to him, but it was obvious they didn't have much in common, and he thought my dad was shirking his responsibility to be my parent. He told me so one night.

"Look, Casey, I'm sorry about the other night," he said and looked me in the eyes. I didn't say anything. "Maybe you didn't hear me, but I called you a lesbian. It was stupid."

"Okay," I said. "Is that why you came here?" I sat down on the other end of the couch.

Steve looked around the room again. "Smells like pipe smoke," he said.

"My grandfather smokes a pipe," I said.

"Oh. That explains it," he said. "Look, um, I don't know what you saw last night, but … um … "

"Steve, I don't care about you and Trevor. It's not my business." Steve looked at me. I wasn't sure what his eyes meant. They just hooked me and held on.

"I mean, I'm not gay. I'm not that way," he said. Suddenly, it felt like Steve and I were the only people on planet Earth sitting on the last couch. The momentary silence was the like the white noise machine Mr. Belner puts on in class when he wants us to do a freewriting exercise. There was sound, but the sound of nothing.

"I don't care," I said because I really didn't care. I could have pulled the phone out of my backpack, where I kept it, and handed it over at that moment, but I guess I didn't want to add to the heightened feeling in the room. Bringing the phone out would essentially be calling Steve a liar because he *was* caught in a romantic position with Trevor. I felt weird, but I held my cards back, as my grandpa would say.

"Look, Trevor and I are friends, and . . ."

"Steve, I don't need an explanation. I really don't."

Steve stood up then and went to the door slowly.

"I am sorry I called you a lesbian," he said.

"It's okay. I am a lesbian."

Fifteen

Martha watched her son closely over the next few
days. He stayed home from school on Monday and Tuesday
claiming his ankle ached so badly that any pressure on it was
painful. On Wednesday, Steve returned to school reluctantly.
She dropped him off on her way to work, and she continued to
think about the words the nurse had whispered to her the night
of the accident. She wanted to bring up the topic, but god, what
exactly was the topic? When she returned home, Steve had dinner
waiting on the table: a rotisserie chicken along with macaroni and
cheese and string beans.

"Steven, what on earth has gotten into you?"

"I can help out my mom, can't I?"

"You most certainly can," she said and sat down to enjoy her
meal. "How was school?"

"Boring," he said.

"Give me more than that."

"It's just really boring. I just want it to be done. I'm tired of
all the bullshit."

"Hey, son, watch your language."

"I'm sorry, but I just feel really stressed out all the time." Martha rubbed Steve's forearm, bit into her chicken, and made an exaggerated happy face.

"Have you heard from the Illinois coach?"

"He left me a message asking me to call him, but I haven't done it yet."

"Why not? That's your scholarship."

"I just feel weird lately."

"Weird how?"

Just then, Steve's phone rang for the third time that evening. It was Carly, and she wanted to come over. He texted her back telling her he didn't feel good.

Steve never answered his mother's question, though Martha probed until she could see she had entered a dead-end street.

Just after dinner, there was a knock at the door. It was Carly. She had come to visit despite Steve's protests.

"Well, come on in, Miss Carly," Martha said. Martha closed the door and began clearing the table. Carly smiled at Steve, who stood up and led her into his bedroom. "Leave the door open, please," Martha called down the hall.

Steve's room was neat and orderly except for an overflowing basket of dirty clothes tucked in the corner next to the closet. His crutches leaned against a desk chair. The curtains were open revealing a parking lot of dark slush and a gray sky. It was nearly seven at night. Carly hugged Steve and then plopped on the bed.

"What's going on with you?"

"What do you mean?"

"You haven't called and you aren't returning my messages. Are you mad at me?"

"No. I'm just having a hard time with my ankle."

"What do you mean?"

"I could lose my scholarship. I'm stressed out."

"Come here," she said and patted the bed next to her. "We need to cuddle."

Steve joined Carly on the bed. She was soft and warm, though he wished she was Trevor, who felt solid and smelled like a pine forest.

"I thought you wanted to break up with me," she said.

"No, but I do feel like I'm having a nervous breakdown."

"That's for forty-year-olds, not teenagers," she said. Steve couldn't help but laugh. They kissed for a while, and then Carly stopped. "You know Connor Cole?"

"Yeah."

"He came up to me at last period today and said that I should be very careful, and he said it really weird, like he knew something that I didn't."

"He's a weirdo," Steve said and hugged her closer.

"I think he should see the school counselor. He's always slinking around. He creeps me out."

"He's always been weird."

"His dad's the chief of police. Maybe that's why he can't relax," Carly said.

"That's not an excuse to spy on people," Steve said.

"What do you mean by that?" Carly cuddled in closer and rubbed Steve's chest.

"I don't know," he said.

"Did he spy on you?"

Steve was quiet for a moment. He couldn't describe the other night and be fully honest.

"Trevor and I were talking the other night, and yeah, he was spying on us. It was weird."

"What?!" Carly sprung up like a cat and blinked several times. Steve laughed.

"That's sooo creepy! What a freak!"

"Yeah. He is totally weird. He barely speaks at practice, and I don't know if I've ever seen him smile," Steve said.

Carly snuggled in as close as she could get. With her head against Steve's chest, she could hear his heart beating fast.

"Are you nervous?"

"No. Why?"

"Your heart is pounding." She looked up at him.

"School's stressing me out. I had a good season, but I gotta keep my grades up."

"This is just a hard time for everybody, Steve. I mean, I'm stressed out, but I still want to be with you."

"Why would you be stressed? You get straight A's. You have your whole life as a scientist planned out. You're set."

Carly was silent for a moment and then sighed heavily. "If I don't get straight A's my parents will disown me, and I never wanted to be a scientist. That was my dad's plan. I've only ever wanted to be an artist, but my parents cried when I told them last summer. They literally both wept."

"Wow!"

"Yeah, Steve, my life is not stress free. We compromised on nutrition—food science. I guess we can all live with that, and maybe I can find some joy in illustrating a nutrition text book." They both laughed then, and Steve squeezed Carly's petite frame.

"Steve, if my parents didn't see me wearing this purity ring, they would not be comfortable with us seeing each other. They'd freak out. Seriously. It's so many damn compromises. I do understand stress. I may smile and laugh a lot, but I have my own shit to handle." Their eyes met, and Steve almost told her everything in that moment, but instead, he just held her.

After Carly left, Martha leaned in the doorway and watched her son read a comic book.

"Is everything okay with you two?"

"Yeah, we're fine," he said.

"Will you answer my question now? Why do you feel weird?"

Sixteen

THAT THURSDAY ROWENA ATE LUNCH WITH TREVOR, STEVE, and Carly. Seemed like old times. She waved to Casey, who sat alone at a small table near the window. Casey waved back. Steve waved too this time, and Casey raised one hand in acknowledgment. Rowena watched Steve and wondered what had transpired to cause that interaction, but she didn't ask or comment. Just quietly noted it. Kids came by to talk and join them and laugh about nothing in particular, and then Connor Cole's tall figure stood above them. He looked at Carly and then at Steve and Trevor. He didn't look at Rowena. He sneered at Steve and mouthed "faggot." Steve jumped up awkwardly and almost lost balance but managed to lunge towards Connor and punch him in the face. Connor screamed, and suddenly a tight circle of kids had formed around the skirmishing boys. Connor tried to yell, but Steve's punches landed hard on his face. Blood spattered up into the air, but he couldn't stop.

Mr. Belner was on lunch duty. He parted the crowd with his massive hands and pried the boys apart. While Mr. Belner attended to Connor, who was blood-covered but not crying, Steve stood back breathing hard and close to tears. The assistant principal arrived, and the four of them left the cafeteria followed by a trail of teenage paparazzi. Phones were front and center followed by loud teenage voices recounting what had just been witnessed like sports commentators after a boxing match. Based on zero knowledge, the consensus seemed to be that Connor got what he deserved.

Carly and Trevor went to the main office to share their side of the attack. Rowena left the building and managed to find a quiet spot in the so-called student smoker's lounge, the old loading dock attached to the east side of the school that was no longer used to receive deliveries. There was no one around when she lit up a Gauloise cigarette, a French cigarette she had become fond of while living abroad. Her mind wandered, still fueled by the adrenaline rush of witnessing violence. Why would Connor approach them like that? Was he just a troubled kid or did he know something about Steve and Trevor? Rowena had wondered herself about their friendship. She and Carly even joked about it from time to time but never seriously.

Rowena's phone pinged loudly. It was a text from Carly asking her to come to the main office. Rowena, being a good friend, stubbed out her cigarette, stood up, took a deep breath, and walked back inside the school building.

Seventeen

WHEN I GOT HOME FROM SCHOOL MY GRANDFATHER WAS IN
good spirits. A box from KFC was on the kitchen table, and he
was pouring lemonade into two glasses filled with ice.

"Been to the chicken farm and brought us dinner on a Thursday
just to mix things up," he said and laughed. He moved slowly,
but his spirits were good, so I relaxed and enjoyed the Colonel's
chicken.

"So how is the schoolhouse treating you, Casey Black?"

"Okay, I guess," I said. What else could I say? I couldn't exactly
unravel the events of the past couple of days and talk about a girl
in my class who had kissed me in the woods. He just stared at me.

"How about a little bit more?" he said and smiled, his old man
liquid eyes fixed on me.

"Life's complicated in high school," is all I could manage.

"That it is. That it is," he said. He coughed hard then and went
into a bit of a coughing jag. He didn't stop until he'd bent over
double and nearly knocked over his lemonade.

"You okay?"

When he sat up, he looked at me and said, "I'm old. I'm a very old man, but I do know when I'm gettin' a half-ass story."

"Well, I'm not quite ready to tell all," I said.

"Okay, but know this: I ain't blind, and I am proud to know you." Then he walked out to the balcony.

"Aren't you gonna finish your food?" I said to the back of his head. I could smell the pipe smoke and knew he wasn't coming back for a while. I cleared the table of our chicken leftovers and went to my room to change into my work clothes. I stood in front of the small mirror on my closet door and smiled. My grandfather was still smoking when I left the house.

Andy wore a red and white Santa hat and waved to me when I walked in. The Wise Owl was busy as usual but not packed. Every table had a little bottle filled with candy canes. There was a mini Christmas tree near the cash register, and flashing red lights had been strung over the front door. After admiring the festive holiday décor and waving to a couple of the regulars, I went directly to the back and started in on the dishes. A Nat King Cole Christmas album replaced Andy's usual eighties music from his high school days, like Duran Duran. Why was everyone's music era the same time they attended high school? It made me think about my character sketch of Larry Dale. He was Andy's age. He must also like eighties music.

Andy shoveled fries into baskets and flipped a burger. His face was sweaty, but he looked happy.

"Happy holidays," Andy said to me and winked.

"I really like what you've done with the place," I said.

"Thanks!"

"Andy?"

"What?"

"Did you go to high school with Larry Dale?"

"Yeah," he said.

"You acted like you didn't even know who he was when he was here before."

"He was a jock and a jerk. I guess I wanted to forget him," he said and walked out to the dining area. I watched him wipe his forehead. I thought about how much had happened at school this week and how life probably gets heavy in your forties because so much life has happened. Maybe too much.

"Are you sad about his daughter missing?"

"Casey, I don't think about him or his daughter or his life." Andy started up two more burgers and dropped some frozen chicken fingers into the fry basket. I focused on doing my dishes, sweeping, mopping, and finally cleaning the bathroom. Before I left, Andy called me over. We were next to the big freezer, and he lifted up his pant leg and showed me an old, red scar that was on the side of his calf.

"See that?"

"Yeah."

"I got that in high school. Your friend Larry shoved me down the stairs in the boys' locker room. I had to get eight stitches. He never apologized and just laughed when I showed him the stitches."

Eighteen

That night was hard. Not because of all the dishes and pots to wash, but because Andy seemed upset about our talk about Larry Dale. He slammed the freezer door shut and aggressively flipped the burgers. His Santa hat had gone crooked. Thirty years seemed like a long time to stay mad at some bully who shoved him down a flight of stairs, but maybe more happened. Maybe Larry tortured him somehow, and he's only willing to show me the one visible scar he has. In history class, we talked a lot about PTSD and how soldiers have suffered the trauma of wars for decades. They used to call it shell shock. If Andy was tortured in some way, maybe he's still mad about it because it left him with an invisible scar too. It was a lot to take in, and I didn't want to stare at him. Overall, he's flexible with me and generally a cool guy. Before I left for the night, I made sure to smile at Andy. He managed to smile and wave back. Blinking red Christmas lights framed him as I took a last look at the café from the sidewalk.

High school can be super hard in ways that no one can prepare you for. Andy got shoved down some stairs by a mean jock, and

I suffered through having to change clothes with a bunch of girls who wore silky, matching bras and panties that emphasized their maturing bodies, while I wore white briefs and undershirts. I tried to appear calm while undressing, but I felt like a total freak and sweated for the solid minute it took to get into my PE uniform. I'm surprised my fro isn't gray by now. Every day was a nightmare in the locker room because I am not a feminine girl, and they don't have a locker room for butch girls who only wear white, cotton, utility briefs. Thank God PE is not required for senior year.

When I turned away from the Wise Owl, I spotted Rowena's beautiful face. She was across the street hugging herself and almost hopping. I guessed to stay warm. She ran across the street and stopped inches from my face.

"Hey, Casey," she said.

"Hi."

A car stopped at the corner stop sign and waited and then drove on. The streets were damp and filled with gray snow slush, but the night was so clear.

"Wanna walk home together?" she asked.

"Sure," I said.

"I was just picking something up from the pharmacy for my mom."

"Oh, okay," I said, not believing her cover story for one minute.

We walked in silence until we were at the end of the street and the edge of the forest. Rowena touched my coat arm, and I turned to her. "What's up?"

"I wasn't really at the pharmacy," Rowena said.

"I kinda figured that," I said with a smile.

We walked into the woods and the snow became deep, and we stumbled and laughed. This time Rowena took me by the arm and held it until I stopped walking.

"Casey, I really like you," was all Rowena said, and then she kissed me full on the mouth. I returned the kiss with a passion that surprised even me. Rowena pulled away from me and stared into my eyes. "You like me too?"

"Yeah."

"Like how do you like me?"

"I like you like a girlfriend."

Rowena stared into my face, and her eyes were soft and accepting. She wanted me too. We kissed again, this time slower with more passion. This was a lover's kiss. She unzipped her coat, took my hand, and placed it under her sweater so that I could feel her naked skin. Our eyes met as my hand found a delicate bra with lace woven throughout. She was so soft. Her hands caressed my hair as I kissed her neck. She closed her eyes, and I watched her head fall back. This was a look of ecstasy. Her cold hands found my naked skin under my coat, and I shivered as she touched me. The soft sounds she made stopped abruptly when we heard a noise. Rowena knelt down beside me, and we waited there in the underbrush, breathing heavily, hearts pounding.

The sounds were the stumbling of a large person who looked like a ship at sea swaying back and forth, moved by an invisible storm within. He crumbled to the ground just several feet away from us.

"Casey, be careful," Rowena said as she crept out behind me. I moved closer and stared down at the unconscious figure. I immediately recognized the tear-stained face and the unkempt thinning hair. He wore the same torn down coat as always, and he smelled like alcohol.

"It's Larry," I whispered.

"Larry who?"

"He's the guy searching for his missing daughter. Remember the flyer I showed you?"

"Should we call 911?"

"I think he's just drunk," I said. I stuck my hands in his pockets and pulled out a crumpled flyer with Patricia's photo on it, a handkerchief, and an old flip phone. I handed the phone to Rowena. "Can you look and see if there's a number for a Daryl in there? That's his brother." Rowena checked his contacts and found Daryl. There were only three other names in the phone. She called Daryl and waited. When a man's voice came on, she handed the phone to me.

Daryl arrived within twenty minutes. During the wait, Rowena and I watched Larry sleep and occasionally snuck kisses. The ground was cold and wet, and we attempted to find suitable seating on a log about ten feet from where Larry slumbered. Daryl was apologetic and thankful. We both assisted him in transporting Larry to Daryl's truck. Larry stumbled and leaned and twisted the whole way back to the roadside. When Larry was finally seated and belted, I asked Daryl about the search for Patricia.

"No clues so far. We're trying not to lose hope, but it's taking a toll," he said and nodded towards his brother, whose chin had sunk to his chest. Heavy, even breaths could be heard in the silence of the night. Daryl drove away and waved. I waved back. Rowena took my hand and we walked back into the darkness of the forest towards the Sky Court complex.

At Rowena's door, I stopped and looked at the only woman I had ever kissed.

"I'm a lesbian," I said.

Rowena laughed.

"So what about you? What're you?"

Rowena's eyes never left mine.

"I don't know what I am, but I know I like being close to you." I nodded my head and started to walk away. Rowena grabbed my arm and moved in close for a final kiss. Just as she did, Trevor swung around the corner holding his nose. He looked scared and lost. He went past quickly without even a nod. I looked at Rowena with raised eyebrows. Rowena shrugged her shoulders, pulled out her door key, and said a final silent goodnight.

Nineteen

TREVOR TRIED TEXTING STEVE FOR THE TENTH TIME THAT evening. He threw the phone on his bed and went to the window after no response. He could hear his dad in the living room watching ESPN, drinking and belching. He wanted to disappear into Steve's muscular arms and close his eyes and leave the world that he knew.

"Trev, get out here! You're missing a good game!" Trevor ignored his dad's call for father-son time. He curled up on the bed in the fetal position and squeezed the phone tight in his hand, willing it to ring or ping. He needed to hear from Steve, damn it!

He found the ancient *Playgirl* magazine Carly had showed him and Steve one night at Steve's place. Carly said she got it at an old woman's garage sale. It had been a joke, and they all laughed at the dudes bearing all for female readers, but Trevor had kept the magazine and hid it under his mattress. He opened to the centerfold picture and laid back. He pulled down his sweatpants, grabbed himself roughly, and began stroking himself while holding the magazine with one hand. The naked man photo spread was a blur by the time he climaxed. He wiped himself off with a sock from the floor and then fell asleep, letting the magazine fall off the bed.

It was around ten when Dean barged into the room and found his teenage son with his sweatpants pulled down. He started to back out and close the door when he spotted the magazine on the floor. He grabbed it quickly, flipped through the pages, and slowly realized what this magazine contained. Sweat beads formed on his forehead and his armpits grew moist. He stared down at Trevor.

"What the hell?" he mouthed. "Trevor! Wake the fuck up!"

Trevor jumped awake and found his father staring at him. He pulled his sweats up and searched for the magazine. Dean dropped the magazine onto the floor and knocked Trevor across the face with the back of his hand.

"What's wrong with you? I thought you were normal? What the fuck is this?"

Trevor's nose began to bleed, and he cried, just sobbed huge tears, but he could not speak. "What's wrong with you? How could you do this to yourself?"

Trevor jumped to his feet and ran past his father, who was shaking his head and cursing louder and louder. He ran from the apartment and swung around the corner with tears stinging his eyes. When he saw Rowena lean into Casey, he walked by quickly.

Twenty

It was nearly midnight when Steve hobbled as quietly as he could out of his apartment, down the stairs, and out into the crisp night. Trevor's plea for help over text had moved him. He'd moped around the apartment all day after his mom left for work, scared to tell her about his suspension from school, the continued pain in his ankle, and the call he'd finally made to the Illinois basketball recruiter who'd delivered some sobering news. Christmas was around the corner, and everything about his life felt hard and inescapable. When he found Trevor huddled in their favorite spot, crying with a dried-up bloody nose, he forgot his problems. He held Trevor close and felt his intense need in the embrace.

"What's going on?"

"My dad knows." Trevor cried as he burrowed his face into Steve's fleece-covered chest.

"Knows about us?"

"He knows about me. He found the *Playgirl* and me with my junk hanging out," he cried.

"Whoa, slow down, what *Playgirl*? What're you talking about?"

"The old, torn up *Playgirl* that Carly showed us."

"That was like two months ago, dude," Steve said.

"I kept it," Trevor said. "My dad found it after I jerked off. I fell asleep."

"Oh shit," was all Steve said. He held Trevor until he finally stopped crying and looked at his face.

"What's gonna happen to us?" Trevor's eyes were big and scared.

Steve didn't say anything because he had no answers. The clear night sky provided only a star-filled vastness that both boys wanted to join.

Twenty-One

It was late when I entered the apartment. My grandfather was in a deep sleep in his bedroom. I needed to do something because I was so revved up from touching Rowena. My mind kept wandering back to her face and lips and nipples. To calm myself down, I focused on my character sketch. It was hard to concentrate, but I did my best. The piece I wrote about Larry wasn't fully factual. It was really more how I perceived him to be. It was stuff I inferred about his life based on what he had told me and what I read in the newspaper and his brother's comments and how he appeared. Seeing him asleep on the cold forest floor gave me something I wasn't expecting. It was almost like he was done, not that he'd given up the search for his daughter, but that he was finished with a part of his life. I needed to see a picture of Larry from his high school days when he played basketball and didn't have a wife or a child. I wanted to see if Larry looked less stressed out. I really hoped he did. I would try to track one down at school tomorrow.

Before I turned out the lamp and fell asleep, I thought about the search. Patricia was a living person who was lost somewhere

or being held captive. It had been several days since her disappearance. If Patricia was alive, it would be a miracle.

In the morning, my grandfather was gone. He left me a note on
the table: *Gone to doctor for a few more tests. See ya when I see ya.
Love, The Old Man.* I tried not to worry too much about him.

I went to school early so I could locate our librarian, Mrs.
Lew. I figured she would be the person to know where all the old
yearbooks were kept. Twenty minutes before first period I found
her in front of her computer in the school library meticulously
typing away with a ceramic mug next to the keyboard. Mrs. Lew
had an almost cold demeanor. Like an obsessed scientist bent on
finding a cure, she rarely wasted time on a greeting. She always
went straight to the point. I wondered what she was like in high
school. Once, though, she made chocolate chip cookies for our
history class when we did library sessions for research last year.
I was as shocked as everybody else.

"Casey, what can I do for you?" I told Mrs. Lew about my character sketch and the need for a yearbook from 1987. She stood
up and went directly into a small, dark room about the size of a
shoe closet and came out with a dark blue yearbook emblazoned
with River City High across the front in big block letters above
a carved print of the school. She handed me the book and went
right back to her desk. I took the yearbook and sat down at a table
near the back of the library.

The kids didn't look that much different than we do today, except in their fashion and hair choices. Maybe a bit more innocent

because they were being photographed, not taking selfies. I'm not sure why I noticed that. Maybe my grandfather was right about all this technology. Maybe it is the devil's work.

I found Larry Dale's picture with the seniors. He had a big smile and a lot more hair. He had on a plaid shirt. I found him again in a photo with the basketball team. He wasn't exactly skinny, but he was a medium-sized guy with, apparently, a lot to smile about. He looked friendly and easygoing. A lot had happened since these photos were taken. I don't know what I thought I was going to learn by looking at his younger face. I also found him in a picture of the Young Entrepreneurs. Larry Dale must have thought he had some business sense back then. Next to him in this picture of mostly boys was Andy, my boss. He smiled too, but he wasn't looking at the camera. He was looking at Larry. Hmmm. I thought Andy hated Larry, but from that picture, it seemed like he felt something other than hate.

When I closed the yearbook, I felt kind of sad. Does everybody go from happy to sad as they age, or do some people get happier as they get older? I gave the yearbook back to Mrs. Lew and left the library wondering about the cumulative impact of life and how it changes your face, your thoughts, and hair. Maybe Mrs. Lew used to smile and laugh a lot too.

The school day was a blur of holiday parties in class and Christmas music blasting over the loudspeakers. Rowena never showed up for English class. I decided to head home before work so I could check on my grandfather and call Rowena. I didn't want to come off as a needy person or a stalker, but I missed her after everything that happened last night. I mean I was a different person. I felt special and wanted, maybe even loved by another human being besides my grandfather.

Back home, there was a small box of chicken on the counter, but no sign of the old man. I went straight to his room and found his bed made and house shoes tucked neatly in front of his dresser. I went back to the kitchen. On the table beneath the chicken box was a note: *Casey, eat this and think of me. I'm at the hospital tending to my lungs. Love, The Old Man.*

I immediately phoned Andy and told him my grandfather was in the hospital and that I'd be in late. He didn't argue with me. I ran down the stairs and out the main drive to Sky Court. I ran as fast as I could to the bus stop and caught the Memorial bus, the bus that runs to the hospital. I sat back in my seat and hugged my backpack to my chest. I wanted to cry. The fact that he had to be admitted to the hospital but still thought to bring me a box of chicken tore at my heart.

He was in room 207. He had the bed next to the window. He didn't have a roommate, so the other bed was empty. The room was very still. My grandfather's hands were folded on his stomach. He turned to look at me and smiled. Then he reached for a switch and raised the top part of the bed so that he was propped up. From the window I could see the sky darkening. It was almost four in the afternoon. I went to my grandfather and hugged him. He had tears in his eyes when he released me from his firm grip.

"What's wrong? What's this all about?" I asked.

"Looks like the boogeyman caught up with me, kiddo," he said and wiped his eyes. He smiled again, showing me his original teeth. I was quiet and waited. "Doctor may want to operate and remove a lung. Says it's got a big tumor in there that's responsible for my crazy coughing and choking."

"When's the surgery?"

"Not sure. We're waiting on the results of some tests. They did x-rays too. They wanna know what they gettin' in bed with," he said.

I set my bag down and squeezed my grandpa's hand. It was hard and bony, the perfect old man hand. My grandpa used to operate a junkyard somewhere on the outskirts of town. His old hands worked hard. I remember visiting as a kid and him yelling at me to be careful and not climb inside the old wrecked autos. I thought it was a car museum.

"But you'll be okay, right?"

"Can't say I will. Can't say I won't," he said and winked.

I tried to smile, but I felt like the rug was being pulled out from under me. I used to hear that saying and not know what people were talking about, but right then I knew exactly what it meant. My world was going to change quickly, and I might lose my footing. My grandfather had been in the Korean War and had smoked a pack a day before switching to a pipe. He'd been married and divorced and then married again to my grandmother and widowed. He'd seen it all. That's what he always said. I think it was true.

A phone rang, and we both jumped. The ringtone was an old telephone ringing, just like ours at the apartment. The sound was coming from my backpack. I must have accidentally turned the mute off on Conner's phone. My grandfather frowned at me.

"Casey Black, I never thought you'd go behind my back and buy a cell phone."

"But I didn't," I said. "I found this in the woods the other day. It's not mine." I dug through my bag until I found the slim silver iPhone. A number appeared on the screen. Then the call went to voice mail.

"You found that fancy phone in the woods?"

"I promise."

"Casey, now is the time when I need you to be the most responsible you ever have been. That gizmo is the devil's work. Get rid of it. You'll see. It'll only take you down a dark path. They were invented to confuse people about life. Get rid of it!"

"Grandpa, calm down. Jesus."

My grandpa slumped back onto his pillows and heaved and then coughed and then held his chest.

"I'm sorry. I promise this phone isn't mine. I'll get rid of it."

His head was nodding that he heard me, but he was still recovering from his coughing fit when two white-coated doctors entered the little room and smiled at me. Before the doctors started to speak, my grandfather pointed to the key ring on his side table. Those were the keys to the Mercury Montego. He rarely let me drive his car because, with only my learner's permit, he was required to ride along. I guess he felt I was ready to drive alone, even though it wasn't legal. He shooed me out, but I stopped just outside the door and listened to the doctors tell him the bad news. I drove home slowly under a dark winter sky.

Twenty-Two

When Martha asked her son why Trevor's big duffel bag and school books were in his room, he told her that Trevor had been fighting with his dad, and things had gotten out of control. Martha knew Dean Morrison had a difficult personality, so she believed her son. She had known Trevor for years and had a strong maternal feeling for the boy, even though she did think he was overly sensitive and clingy towards her son at times. When Steve asked if Trevor could stay with them Friday and over the break, she said yes.

Dean Morrison arrived at the apartment just after nine in the morning. Trevor had gone to school. Steve had gone to the public library due to his suspension. It was Friday before break, but for Martha this was the start of her three days off. When she heard the knock at the door, she was brewing coffee and listening to soft jazz. She sighed and reluctantly went to open the door. This was supposed to be her time.

"Hey, Martha," Dean said.

"Dean," she said and stood firmly in the doorway. Dean's face was unshaven and bristly, just like his personality. Over the years they'd had some words, but Martha still had sympathy for him. She knew he had a bad back and had never stopped grieving for his dead wife. Knowing the origin of his daily anger and frustration softened her a bit, but she still found him a challenge, and she knew him to be a selfish man.

"Look, I know Trevor's staying here."

"He is," she said, unmoving.

"I ... um ... I need to talk," he said and looked down at the concrete floor. His demeanor was uncharacteristic of the man who once got so mad he broke a chair at a PTA meeting. Martha stepped aside and allowed him to enter her home. Dean walked in like a shy teenager. He looked at the apartment that was painted in a pastel yellow. The couch had pillows on it, and the windows had curtains, not blinds. There were flowers on the table, and he smiled at the music.

"Chet Baker," he said. "I have this album too."

"It's soothing," Martha said. "How about some coffee?"

"That'd be great," he said.

He sat down gently on the couch. Dean smiled but felt a bit uncomfortable in such a feminine home. It made him think of Linda and how she had sewed curtains for their old place near the lake. She'd sewn pillow covers for all the pillows, and even made stuffed animals for the boys from old material scraps. She'd really made the old hunting cabin snug and homey feeling. When he and the boys had moved into Sky Court, he'd been at a loss as to how to recreate that feeling of home and love, so he didn't dare try. The love left with Linda, and he'd become a bully.

Martha reappeared and handed him a mug of hot coffee. Dean took it and sipped. His face relaxed.

"Look, Martha, the reason I'm here is because, the other night, Trevor and I got into it pretty bad. Maybe I jumped to conclusions. I mean he is just a teenager, but it scared me, and I freaked out. I'd been drinking, and I just didn't get it. I mean he's into sports and likes to go fishing and…I just…I guess I'm lost," he said rapid-fire. Martha frowned. She had no idea what he was talking about. Seeing her confused face, Dean unfolded the *Playgirl* he'd rolled up in his fist and placed it between them on the couch. Martha looked at the magazine. A handsome, half-naked man adorned the cover.

"Dean, I don't read this magazine. I'm really confused about why you're here," she said. Dean opened the magazine to the nude male centerfold and held it out so that Martha could take it all in. "I've seen naked men before, Dean. What's your point?"

"Trevor! Trevor was jerking off to this!" Dean threw the magazine down onto the floor and buried his face in his hands. "What does this mean?"

Martha picked up the magazine, put the centerfold back in its place, and set it down on the coffee table.

"Dean," she said and touched his arm instinctively. "This does not mean that Trevor is gay. It could mean that, but it may not, and even if he is, what's the big deal?"

"What's the big deal?" Dean stared at Martha as if she were a Martian.

"What if he is attracted to men instead of women? He's still Trevor, the same kid who likes basketball and fishing," she said.

"What if this was Steve we were discussing? Would you be so fucking calm about it?"

Martha glared at Dean, who quickly apologized for his language.

"Dean, I've had my suspicions about my own son. He has never said anything to me one way or the other. If he did tell me he was gay, I honestly wouldn't be that surprised. He seems much happier in the company of Trevor than Carly." Dean was silent for a while. "I want Steve to be happy in his own skin and with his life. He's my son, but he's not me. He has to make his own life choices. He's almost eighteen. He's gonna leave home next year."

Dean stared out the window. The clear night sky had clouded over early in the morning, and now a heavy grayness threatened to dump more snow on River City.

"Maybe it's different for fathers," he said. "I thought you'd be on my side."

"I'm not on a side, Dean. What are you so upset about?"

"Martha, I cannot imagine wanting a man sexually," he nearly yelled.

"You are not Trevor," Martha said.

When Dean walked out of the apartment with the heavy footsteps of defeat, Martha walked to Steve's room and examined the tiny bedroom painted a medium blue and covered with posters and pictures of professional basketball players in motion. She sat on his bed and ran her fingers over the old wool blanket she'd bought so many years ago at a military surplus store. Steve wouldn't relinquish it even though it had torn in several places and looked as if it had survived a war. She saw Trevor's bag on the floor at the foot of the bed and wondered if the two friends were, in fact, lovers.

Twenty-Three

Rowena sat in the smoker's lounge alone again and shivered in the cold. The old loading dock felt like a refuge from the hormone-charged high school students she would have to endure for one last semester. There was talk of an online senior year program, but the school board seemed to be deliberating forever. If it passed, she would definitely do her final semester online.

She could hear the screams and yells from the track field. The cheerleaders were practicing early because of the threat of more snow. She wished they'd stayed in the gymnasium. She rolled her eyes at the memory of her own cheerleader life just a short year ago. Now it all seemed like a distant dream. Before her adventure abroad, she enjoyed two parents, getting crushes on boys, and eating burgers and fries. A year later, she had only a mother to rely on, no more boy crushes, and she was an aspirational vegetarian. She thought about Casey way too much. She wrote about her in her journal every night and went out of her way to walk past the Wise Owl after school to see if she could see her. Whenever she was in a class she hated, like trigonometry, she would think about Casey kissing her, and she would smile and survive class. Their touching the night before had become her favorite memory. She wondered if Casey was as obsessed with her, and she hoped she was. She wanted to be nonchalant, but the feelings were all there. They could not be denied.

"Hey, Ro!" Carly shouted and walked over to the loading dock. Carly looked seriously at her friend. The girls hugged, and Carly sat down next to Rowena, who offered her the cigarette. Carly took it and sat back. "School's weird without Steve," she said and ran her fingers through her shiny black hair.

"What about Connor? Was he suspended too?" Rowena asked.

"I don't know about him. He probably got off," she said and sucked in more fragrant cigarette smoke.

"But he provoked him."

"He called him a faggot, or something. I didn't actually hear anything, but Steve said that. The assistant principal didn't think name calling was justification for Steve's reaction, so Steve is gone for the day."

"Wow," Rowena said. "Why do you think Connor did it? I mean they don't really know each other."

Carly thought about that. The air was cold and dry. She looked out at the empty girls' soccer field in front of them. It was a mess and needed to be cared for properly. Just beyond the soccer field was a fallow field with brittle, twisted, forgotten corn stalks bent from the wind, snow, and ice. The dark scene depressed her.

"I don't know. Connor's always been kind of a weird one. I mean he just keeps to himself. I don't even know why he's on the basketball team. I mean he's tall and coordinated, I guess, but he never plays, just sits there on the bench every game. I think he's jealous of Steve. I think he needs help."

Rowena studied her friend who loved to laugh and joke around but was actually a very serious person. She once confided to Rowena that it was not easy being the only Chinese person in a small Midwestern high school.

"You're probably right. It can't be easy having your dad be chief of police," Rowena said. The squeals of the out-of-sight cheerleaders grew, and finally Rowena and Carly began laughing at their noise. They laughed so hard they doubled over and hit their heads together and just kept laughing.

Twenty-Four

"Casey, I wasn't expecting you after yesterday's news," Andy said. His Santa hat sat on the counter, and now Dean Martin crooned more Christmas songs. He had the dishwasher running and was cooking three burgers. I threw on my apron and went to the sink. "How's your grandfather today?"

"He's getting more tests done. His lungs are struggling. He may need surgery," I said as I dove into work. I wanted to keep busy. I'd skipped English class at the end of the day because I didn't want Rowena to see my stressed-out face. I mean, I wanted to just curl up with her, but I also didn't want to seem needy. I'd just gone back to the apartment and sat on my grandfather's bed. I'd closed my eyes and imagined life on my own. This was painful. I didn't want a smoke-free apartment without old man wisdom.

"You don't have to be here right now. I can handle things tonight," he said over the noise of the dishwasher.

"I know, but Friday nights are always busy. Anyway, I didn't want to be at home thinking sad thoughts."

"Okay," he said and flipped the burgers. He left me alone for the rest of the night, and I was glad when business picked up. I stayed busy until eight, and when I wrapped up, I was tired. My brain was empty. I felt good. Andy nodded to me as I headed for the door. He liked to do the books at the counter, and I could see his profile as he crunched numbers and sipped coffee. Seeing him sitting there made me think of the Young Entrepreneur's photo and Larry Dale. They must have been friends or had some kind of connection, or maybe Andy had just admired Larry. Andy looked up at me. "You okay?"

"Yeah. I . . . "

"You've got a lot on your mind, Casey. It's okay if you want time off," he said before I could ask him about Larry. I thought twice about it.

"No. I'm okay," I said and walked out of the little café.

The green neon sign blinked out, and I walked to the Mercury Montego parked in the lot across the street. It felt strange climbing onto the cold, vinyl seat and starting a car. I had never driven home from work. I started the car and turned on the heater. I just sat there for a moment, and then I saw Rowena walk in front of the café. She was smoking and walking real slow. She peered into the front window then walked on. I pulled out of the lot and drove onto the street next to her. She jumped and then smiled when she saw it was me following her. I opened the passenger door, and she flicked her cigarette into a snow drift and jumped in.

"Whose car?"

"My grandfather's," I said. "He's in the hospital."

"Oh, is he okay?"

"I don't know yet," I said.

"Missed you in English class," she said and rubbed my thigh.

I drove us through the small town and up to the peak. I'd never been to the peak, but I knew where it was, and I'd always wondered what it would be like to drive up there with a girlfriend and get close. I made a mental note to get my license as soon as my grandpa gets home. No more breaking the law. A learner's permit is only halfway to the goal. I drove past a couple of cars that I recognized from school and kept going until I reached the little turnoff that Larry had told me about. It was just a dip after a sudden left turn, and there was really only room for one large car or two compact cars. I pulled in and parked. Rowena looked at me and smiled. She rolled down her window and sucked in some frigid air and blew it out.

"This is where Trevor and Steve got hit by Larry," I said.

"How do you know?"

"Larry told me. He left the scene and came to the café and told me the whole story," I said.

Rowena unbuckled herself and moved in close to me. She leaned against me and wrapped my arms around her. She smelled so good.

"Were you looking for me at the café when I spotted you?" I asked.

"Yeah," she said and kissed me on the neck. She snuggled in, and I squeezed her tight. I kissed her back, and soon we were in a tight embrace. That's when I saw the lights. There were maybe twenty flashlights below us on the low sloping hill where Steve's little car must have rolled to after being struck. The flashlights resembled a pack of huge fireflies drifting through the field.

"What's going on?" Rowena asked.

"That's a search party. They're looking for Patricia. I should be with them," I said.

"Why?"

"I said I'd help." Rowena took my face in her hands and kissed me hard on the mouth. She opened her mouth, and I tasted her tongue. *I love this girl*, I thought.

Twenty-Five

BARBARA STOOD AT THE SINK AS HER DAUGHTER SAT AT THE table sipping coffee and dreamily munching on a buttered piece of baguette. The early morning light drifted in through the window. A light snow had begun to fall.

"You got in kinda late last night, honey. Everything okay?"

"Yeah. I'm fine," Rowena answered. Barbara sat down across from her daughter, who seemed to have become a stranger in recent months. She touched Rowena's hand and smiled.

"I know this divorce and all the crap between your dad and me have been hard for you, but I'm still here for you," she said.

"I know, Mom."

"Well, what's going on, baby? We used to share a lot, and now it's like your life is one big secret."

Rowena looked into her mother's eyes. She saw a tired, middle-aged woman who hadn't had a job for decades. Her mom had put up with years of abuse from her dad, and she felt a pang of guilt because secretly she sometimes missed her dad's presence. When he wasn't being cruel to her mother, he could be funny, and he often talked to her about serious adult issues that made her feel like a grown-up. Once, late at night, he'd told her that he'd had an affair with his administrative assistant but had broken things off. She had never revealed this to her mother, but felt sickened that she knew this information about her father. Why had he told her? He'd said he needed to get it off his chest. She had only listened and told him she was glad it was over. He seemed relieved, but when she went to bed that night, she cried, and she felt confused for days. She both hated and loved her father, and now she was alone with this woman, who was her mother, but who needed protecting.

"Mom, school is rough right now. I don't want to be there, but I want to graduate, so I'm doing all I can to just get through."

"High school should be fun, baby, not a chore," her mother said.

"Well, it feels like a chore," she said. "Was it fun for you?"

Barbara thought hard for a moment. "Some of it was. I think kids are different these days. I had a lot of work when I was a teenager helping my mom with the other kids. Plus I worked at a dairy after school until night. I guess we just led different lives. I wanted your high school days to be fun, honey. Boy troubles?"

"Boy troubles?" Rowena said. "I don't have a boyfriend, and I don't want one."

"Well, okay, but you used to laugh more, and I still don't really understand why you quit cheerleading," her mother said.

"Mom, I'm growing up. I'm sorry. I'm gonna go meet Carly at the mall." Barbara watched her independent daughter get up from the table and walk down the hall. She blamed herself and her bad marriage for Rowena's lack of joyfulness. She finished her coffee and pulled out the newspaper. She went straight to the Jobs section in the classifieds of the *River City Current*.

Twenty-Six

With Trevor out running an errand for her, Martha wondered if this was the right moment to approach her son about the fight at school. Steve had his leg propped up on a pillow and laid back on the couch engrossed in *The View*, a show that Martha found annoying but was touched somehow that Steve enjoyed listening to the opinions of middle-aged women. Steve had taken his suspension easily. He didn't care. He felt discouraged about life at the moment, and the suspension was just one more additional hiccup.

"Steven, we need to talk," Martha said as she joined him on the couch. He looked at her and turned the volume down on the TV. "Let's turn that off for now," she said. Steve obeyed his mother and tossed the remote onto the coffee table. She looked at his ankle. Steve sat up straighter on the couch. When his eyes met hers, he immediately began crying. Martha, startled, grabbed her son and pulled him close. Steve cried on and didn't resist his mother's hold. "What's wrong, son?"

"I think I lost it," he cried.

"Lost what?"

"My scholarship to Illinois," he finally managed to get out. Martha squeezed him tightly. This was not the conversation she had planned on. Through fat tears, Steve revealed that he had spoken to the Illinois recruiter, and that based on the extent of his injury, the scholarship may be in jeopardy.

"But you signed a letter of intent," she said.

"I know, Mom. These are NCAA rules. They're allowed to do this. The recruiter spoke to my doctor. I signed that release giving him a right to my medical records."

"It's only been a couple of weeks. You're still healing, baby."

Steve finally sat back and regained composure. He wiped his face with the sleeve of his long-sleeved t-shirt. To Martha, Steve still resembled a tall, gangly kid with an infectious smile and laugh. She wanted to protect him, but he was not a child.

"Is it too late to reach out to the community college team that offered you their scholarship?"

"I don't know," he said, suddenly seeming out of reach again. Martha felt the closeness had passed. She remembered why she sat down.

"Steven, you never fully explained to me why you beat up Connor Cole."

Steven looked away. He stared into the lights of the Christmas tree that Martha had only set up two days before. She looked at it and smiled because she was notoriously late when it came to decorating the house for the holidays. She admitted to herself that when Steve left for college, she probably wouldn't go further than throwing a wreath on the front door. Holidays had never been easy for her growing up poor, and not much had changed while Steve's father had been in her life.

"He called me a name," he finally said in a flat quiet voice.

"What name was that?" Martha reached out for Steve's hand, but he pulled away and stood up. He reached for his crutches and hesitated for a moment. His eyes met his mother's and he adjusted his crutches and slowly left the room. Martha wanted to pursue the conversation, but she was tired, and some part of her felt like Steve's tears were breakthrough enough for one day.

Twenty-Seven

TREVOR CARRIED MARTHA'S DRY CLEANING THROUGH THE
cold morning air. He didn't know when or if he could go back
to his own apartment. He thought his dad might beat him if he
set foot in there again. He felt stressed and walked faster to stay
warm when he spotted Rowena on the corner.

The light changed, but Rowena didn't move. He caught up
with her just as she lit up a cigarette. Her mind was on Casey and
how nice it felt to be held in her arms. Casey was sweet, smart,
and a damn good kisser. She smiled remembering their time
together. Trevor tapped her on the shoulder.

"Why are you smiling?" he asked. She looked surprised.

"I don't know," she said. Rowena and Trevor had never been
completely alone together. Trevor reached out for her cigarette.
She took it and handed it to him. She lit up another one for herself.

"What are these? They kinda smell like a cigar."

"They're French," she said. "Gauloise." She held up the blue
flip top pack so he could read the name. "Why do you have dry
cleaning?"

"Oh, this stuff belongs to Steve's mom," he said.

He inhaled and then blew smoke out. He looked down at the recently shoveled sidewalk. Rowena watched him. He had thick eyelashes and shaggy hair. His corduroys hung low on his tiny hips, and he seemed small to her even though he was six feet tall. His letter jacket was old. He didn't wear gloves. He had a mole on his neck.

"I'm in trouble," he finally said.

"What kind of trouble?"

The wind picked up quickly, making the cold air even colder, but neither of them made to go anywhere. Rowena just watched his soft brown eyes.

"My dad hates me because he found a *Playgirl* magazine in my room. He thinks I'm gay."

"Are you?" Rowena asked.

Twenty-Eight

I SAT IN MY GRANDPA'S CAR IN THE HOSPITAL PARKING LOT because I wasn't quite ready to face things. I'd let Andy know that I might be late for work. He told me to do whatever I needed to do. I turned off the heater and cut the ignition. I stepped out of the car, locked the door, and walked into the River City Hospital.

When I reached room 207, the door was open. Two nurses walked out past me, and then a doctor in a white coat followed. Nobody stopped to say anything to me. I walked in and found my grandfather sitting up. His breathing was labored. He tried to smile through gasps, and I moved in close to him and took his hand. His grasp was strong. He coughed hard and then pulled me close to him. He tried to speak but coughed again. Finally, he managed to control his breathing. He smiled as if he was okay, and he said, "Young one, walk yo walk." He closed his eyes and let his head fall back. He looked peaceful. His heart monitor was beeping normally, so I relaxed. I sat down in a chair near the bed and watched his bald head move about on the pillow. He fell into a deep sleep.

Without realizing it, I fell asleep too. When I sat up and blinked awake, I could see my grandpa was still sleeping. It was nearly eight at night. I stood up, stretched, and walked to the window. More snow, and it looked beautiful. I hugged my grandfather goodbye, even though he couldn't hug me back, and left the hospital.

The Montego started right up, and I drove to the Wise Owl. I parked in the lot across the street and was about to cross over when I saw Connor Cole leaving the café through the kitchen's back door. He was carrying a large takeout bag. That was odd. I waited until he was down the street to cross over.

Andy was standing by his tiny desk that is crammed in the back corner of the kitchen in an alcove next to the pantry. He looked scared. I had never seen his face look so stressed. He had new forehead lines.

"Andy?"

"Casey, I thought you weren't coming in," he said.

"My grandfather's sleeping. I needed to do something," I said.

"Well, as you can see, the dishes waited for you," he said and attempted to smile, but it didn't work. His face reminded me of Larry Dale's face when he first came in that snowy night and told me about his crash. I didn't want to mention Connor at that point, so I put on my apron and got to work. Andy watched me and then asked after my grandfather, but it was more out of politeness than caring. He was obviously preoccupied.

"He's struggling," was all I said.

The night went by fast. Business picked up along with the snow, and I kept up a steady pace of washing dishes, wiping down tables, sweeping. When I took the mats outside to hose them down, the snow was coming faster, and it was sticking to the street. I'd have to drive slow going home. I looked up at the sky and then noticed a light on in a window above the pharmacy. A curtain closed quickly, and I couldn't help but wonder if that was Andy's secret lover. Maybe she thought that he would be washing the kitchen mats, and she could spy on her lover while he worked. I dragged them back inside and hung them over three chairs I clumped together. I mopped the floor and then grabbed my backpack. I waved goodbye to Andy, who waved back and said something, but I couldn't hear him beneath the Johnny Mathis Christmas album that he had cranked up after the last customer left.

The apartment felt empty when I dropped my bag on the floor near the door and walked to the fridge. I found the box of KFC from the other day and forced myself to eat a piece of chicken. As I ate it, I thought about my grandfather calling it the chicken farm. I smiled.

The sound of Connor's cell phone jarred me back to the present moment. I'd left the phone in my room on my bookshelf. I went to grab it, but it had stopped ringing and the call had gone to voice mail. I put the phone back on the shelf and stared at it for a moment. Maybe I should throw it away. That's what I was told to do. I couldn't though. I felt like it was important.

I spent the rest of the night finishing up my paper about displacement. It was not hard to write. I didn't want to be in my bed, so I grabbed my blanket and pillow and crashed on the couch. Maybe my grandfather would surprise me and walk through the front door in the morning with a bag of donuts. I fell asleep hoping for the best.

Twenty-Nine

DEAN MORRISON SAT AT THE KITCHEN TABLE DRINKING coffee and reading the paper. He was unusually sober this Christmas Eve and had straightened up the apartment and washed his and Trevor's bed sheets. He was about to bundle up the newspapers for recycling when he read the headline: *Missing Girl's Doll Stolen*. He had been mildly interested in the Patricia Dale case because he knew Larry from the occasional truck driving work he did that didn't interfere with his VA disability wages. They'd run into each other from time to time, grabbed a beer once or twice. They'd never been friends, but they were certainly acquaintances. The story stated that Chief Cole released new and startling information about a recent doll theft from Patricia Dale's grandparent's home. Katrina and Larry were separated, and Katrina and Patricia had been staying with Katrina Dale's parents, the Lassiters, who also reside in River City. Dean shook his head in bewilderment. The front-page article seemed to imply that Patricia was still alive. He couldn't follow the logic, but hoped that she was still breathing.

When he finished his coffee, he took all the newspapers out to the recycling dumpster, where he bumped into Martha Jones. Martha hugged herself tightly in a long wool sweater and stood beneath the roof of the semi-enclosed garbage and recycling area. It was already dark. Dean thought the day had gotten away from him until now.

"Hey, Martha, how's it going?"

"I'm okay, Dean. Are you feeling better?"

"I don't know. I did clean my house though," he said and laughed. Martha laughed too. "Wanna have a cup of coffee?" Dean surprised himself by asking, and was even more surprised when Martha said yes.

The apartment was sparse but orderly with a battered couch and a chair that faced each other. There were no Christmas ornaments anywhere. The chair was by the wall. Behind it was a beautiful landscape painting that drew Martha in. She walked closer to it while Dean prepped the coffee in the tiny kitchen.

"Do you take cream and sugar?" Dean's voice brought her back to the fact that she was in this man's apartment.

"Oh, yes, please." Dean took his time making the coffee. He said it was the best thing he made, and Martha laughed. When Dean handed her the old mug, she noticed his rough, scarred hands, and he noticed her looking.

"Work. My hands. It's from work. I grew up lumberjacking with my dad in Oregon, then a stint in the Army. That's when my back got jacked up lugging an eighty-pound pack on my hundred-seventy-pound frame. Bad math. Anyway, after that there was truck driving, fishing in Alaska, and then welding train track.

I'm beat up, Martha. If I hadn't got that VA disability claim that I fought for, I couldn't work enough now to feed those boys. I'm just a beat up old man." He laughed. Martha just smiled.

"How are you feeling about Trevor now?"

As he sat down beside Martha on the couch, he felt a bit embarrassed by his home after his visit to her cozy apartment.

"I've cooled down, I guess, but I don't get it. I mean, Trevor was a normal kid. I just want him to stay normal and have a regular life."

"Dean, being gay isn't abnormal. Some people are gay and some are straight. It's pretty simple." Dean shook his head. He didn't want to accept what Martha was saying, but he liked the company. He enjoyed having a woman's smell in his dingy apartment. They talked for a few more minutes, and then Martha finished her coffee and set her mug on the coffee table.

"That was good. Thank you. Excellent," she said.

"Told you I could make great coffee. That's one thing I do know how to do really well."

Martha looked at Dean and thought she saw tears in his eyes, so she stood up, walked quickly to the door, and opened it to let herself out. Before stepping out into the hallway, she turned and called, "Merry Christmas." She thought she heard Dean say it back to her as she stepped away from the door.

Thirty

Steve and Trevor were adding more to the hastily dec-orated tree that Martha had pulled out of a box from the storage unit. Steve always asked for a real tree, but Martha knew once she set up the artificial tree, he'd be happy.

"How long are you gonna be mad at your dad?" Steve asked.

"Why? You want me to leave?"

"No, dumbass. I'm just wondering. I mean you can't stay mad forever."

Trevor hung a small black angel on a branch and stared at Steve. Steve stared back.

Steve wanted to help Trevor survive, but a part of him wanted to keep him at a distance. Trevor's neediness felt like too much for him to handle while he was trying to figure out what to do about school and his precarious scholarship. His ankle throbbed, and the crutches he wanted to be rid of had become critical.

"I don't know. He hates me," he said. "He hates me for being gay."

"You're not gay, Trevor."

"I'm not? We have sex, Steve. I know I'm gay."

Steve walked into the kitchen and poured a large glass of orange juice and drank it. Trevor walked in after him and touched his arm.

"When I'm not with you, I want to be. You're all I think about," Trevor said.

Steve turned away and placed his glass in the sink.

"Steve, I love you. Do you love me?"

Steve returned to the tree and found another decoration to hang.

"Steve?"

Trevor's pleading voice was making Steve sick

"Trevor, shut up. You sound like a girl."

Trevor stormed into the bedroom and slammed the door. Steve continued to hang ornaments. Martha walked in and smiled at her son.

"Everything okay?"

"Yep."

"Where's Trevor?"

"He was tired and crashed."

Martha looked down the hall and walked into the kitchen. Steve started to put away the remaining ornaments while Martha faced the dishes. Steve walked into the kitchen and watched his mom. She smiled at him, and he wanted to talk but wasn't sure how to start.

"What's up, chicken butt?" This made Steve laugh. He softened inside.

"Thanks for not getting mad about the scholarship," he said.

"Steven, your injured ankle isn't your fault. Accidents happen, and we don't know for sure what's gonna happen yet with Illinois," she said.

"I'm gonna call that community college coach after vacation."

"I think that's a good idea," she said.

"Goodnight, Mom."

"Goodnight, son."

Steve entered the darkness of his small bedroom. The lights were off. Trevor's sleeping bag was on the floor, but he wasn't in it. Steve went to his bed and found Trevor tucked under the blankets.

"What are you doing?"

"I want you, Steve." Trevor pulled back the blankets revealing his fully naked self. He smiled in the darkness. Steve undressed slowly and then climbed in the twin bed next to him. Trevor's skin was warm and soft. They were very quiet.

Thirty-One

My grandfather died Christmas morning. I received the phone call from his doctor just before seven. The ringing woke me. I sat up on the couch and reached for the old black rotary phone. The doctor had a heavy voice that delivered the news slowly, methodically. I could hear the fatigue and sadness in his report. I hung up and just sat there.

The phone rang about ten minutes later, but I didn't pick it up. I let my grandpa's ancient answering machine get it. I sat still and listened to a woman from the hospital, a social worker, inform me when the body could be collected. She also gave me the name and number to the local funeral home. She said something about forms having to be signed by an adult, and she asked my age. I sat very still for about thirty minutes, then I rose from the couch to use the toilet. I think I was in shock. I sat on the toilet feeling overwhelmed with the list of tasks that had to be completed. I kept rubbing my mashed-down fro. Maybe this is why my grandfather always rubbed his bald head — to think better. Everything would be closed on Christmas, so I stepped into the shower and let the warm water soothe me. I made the water hotter and hotter until I couldn't stand it anymore, and then I shut it off. That's when I cried. Just crumpled onto the tile floor and howled. For the first time in a long time I wished an adult was in my life who could step in and handle all the details, talk to the hospital people, fill out forms, pay for services, and tell me what to do. Why did I have to be so alone in all of this? I got up from the floor and dried off with my towel. I walked to the couch and sat down and cried until I had nothing left.

I called my dad and got his voice mail. I choked out a please call me. I didn't think telling him that his father had died was okay to leave in a message. I slept on the couch for several hours, and when I woke up, the day was gray and still heavy. It was hard to imagine my grandfather alone on a slab in the hospital morgue. But he was alone just like me. I saw the red blinking light on the ancient answering machine. I must have slept through the call. I pressed play and heard my dad saying Merry Christmas. His voice wasn't very merry. I played it one more time and then got up and pulled on some clothes. I wasn't hungry, so I went to the kitchen table and completed my character sketch of Larry Dale. With both assignments done, I wasn't sure what to do, so I made some coffee and waited. I should have called my father back. He was an adult who could step in and help me, but I didn't call. I felt disconnected from him and his sad voice. In that moment I felt grown up. Maybe being grown is about facing things you really don't want to but just getting on with it because, if you don't, nobody else will. Maybe this is why Andy and Larry have tired eyes and gray hair.

A visitor at the door interrupted my thoughts. The knock was hard, so I jumped off my chair and hurried to the door.

"Rowena?" She had on a green sweater and jeans. She walked in with big, shiny eyes.

"Merry Christmas," she said. She had never come over before, so this felt strange.

"My grandfather died this morning," I said.

She threw her arms around me and squeezed me hard. I didn't cry though. We moved to the couch. She kissed me and murmured things in my ear. Her breath smelled like spearmint gum.

"I'm so sorry, Casey," she said. Her big brown eyes felt like a blanket of love. I stroked her hair and face and just took all of her in.

"I came because my dad stopped by, and my mom decided to be nice to him, which is bizarre because he has been known to get violent. She has a restraining order against him right now."

"Adults are strange," I said, thinking about my dad and his fake happy voice. I still needed to let him know about his father, but I couldn't call him back. I put his face out of my mind. Rowena moved in closer, and the day merged into evening as we explored each other. We fell asleep in the dark.

In the morning Rowena was gone. I was on the couch in my underwear and a t-shirt. The night was fuzzy. The blinds were open, and the snow drifted down from the sky lazily but persistently. Christmas was over. Nothing about the day before felt like a holiday. I stood up and walked into my grandfather's bedroom.

His bed was neat. His house slippers were parked right in front of his dresser. His licorice pipe smoke smell still perfumed the room. A photo of him and another guy in the Army sat on top of his dresser. At the bottom of the picture, it was stamped KOREA. My grandfather looked sweet and gentle even in his Army uniform. I started to cry again and collapsed on his bed. I burrowed my face into his pillow. I wanted my friend back.

I rose when I heard Conner's cell phone ringing. I walked down to my room and picked up the slim silver phone. There was that same number. I put the phone back on the shelf and went to shower. Now that the holiday was over, I would need to take care of grandpa's remains.

The rest of the morning was a blur. I had to lie about my age to sign papers in the hospital. I would turn eighteen in four months, so I didn't worry about the legality of it all. I'd called the number the lady from the hospital had given me and arranged for transport. A man in a dark suit and tie loaded my grandfather into a vehicle to take him to the crematorium. I drove home and found the box of tobacco in my grandfather's bedroom. I knew exactly what I was to do.

My grandfather had shown me the tobacco box last year and revealed the hidden compartment. "Just in case," he'd said and winked at me. We never mentioned it again, so I knew what I was looking for when I entered his room and first spotted his house shoes. They made me want to cry, but I didn't. I was in full adult mode. I took the old tobacco box, lifted up a fake bottom, and found a stash of bills. I counted the money. He had over six thousand dollars. The crematorium man said the cost was eight hundred dollars. I brought money back to the crematorium and paid a woman in a blue blouse who wore a lot of red lipstick. "Sorry," she said.

I got to see my grandfather's face one last time before they placed him into a container and shoved him into the oven. He looked like a distinguished stranger with closed eyes, but that shiny, bald head was very familiar. I couldn't quite grasp the fact that this man would never bring home Kentucky Fried Chicken ever again. It all just happened so fast. I held his old Black hand one last time and traced the raised veins. A lever was thrown, and he disappeared into the darkness of the oven. A man in a shirt and tie told me to come back in a few days, and I would get an urn with the remains. So that's life.

I said okay and left. I wanted to go to work to lose my brain in the rhythm of dishwashing, but I was too exhausted and hungry. I drove to the local Chinese restaurant, The Golden Lotus, and ordered Mongolian beef with rice and egg rolls. I drove home and put the food on the counter and sat on the couch. I knew I should call my dad and inform him that his father had died, but I felt worn out. I picked up the heavy black receiver and dialed his number. I got the voice mail again, so I hung up without leaving a message. I laid back on the couch and closed my eyes. I slept for hours.

Part Two

Thirty-Two

ON CHRISTMAS MORNING, CONNOR COLE BENT HIS LONG LEGS and kneeled down near the heater vent in his room. He put his ear against the wall, leaned in, and listened. The heating vents in the house moved not only warm air into the rooms but also voices. He could hear his parents talking in the kitchen while he remained in his bedroom upstairs. His father dropped some silverware. He could hear it land on the old pine floor. He couldn't see her, but he could imagine his mother bending down to pick it up and hand it back to his father, who would wait patiently until the silverware was returned.

Connor and his father never got along. Connor knew his father to be a hard man who grew up in a family of lawmen and lawwomen from Wyoming. He'd heard so many stories from his dad and knew his life had just been sixty-seven years of harshness. Connor's bother, Paul, had been like their father. Unquestioning, ready to serve. Connor was a gentle kid, a daydreamer who was always open and smiling, traits his father didn't know how to handle. As Connor grew older, he grew distant from his father, letting a cloud of silence shield him from his family. Only Paul could break through the cloud and make him laugh. With Paul's death, the cloud became an impenetrable fog.

Connor heard his mother speak, and he pressed as close to the vent as he could get. The warm air oozing from the metal vent made him sleepy, but he had to stay alert. He had to know how the investigation was progressing. His father rarely spoke in front of him about police business, though he told his mother everything.

"So what about the doll? Were any fibers left behind? Anything?" his mom asked.

"I already told you we have nothing. The break-in at the Lassiter's is difficult because they said they never lock their doors. A neighbor kid could conceivably have walked in off the damn street, seen the doll, and walked off with it. We just don't know."

"But you canvassed the neighborhood?"

"Of course we did. Nothing was found!"

"Calm down, dear."

"I can't. This has gone on too long. It doesn't make sense."

"Well, how's Larry handling everything?"

"He's not doing well, according to Daryl."

"Poor thing."

"Yeah, he's a disaster, and he hasn't exactly been ruled out of suspicion."

"I thought he was working the night she disappeared."

"Well, that's true, but he drives a truck. No one drives with him. He crashed that box truck the same day she disappeared. There's still a lot of unanswered questions. His work alibi isn't airtight."

Connor stood up and walked to his bed. He lifted the mattress and stared down at the doll with blond curly hair and a green dress on. It was a simple, plain doll. Nothing fancy.

Later in the day, Connor skipped dinner despite his parents' protest. He wanted to avoid his father's watchful eyes, and he had spent enough time with them earlier opening presents and watching "It's A Wonderful Life" on TV. Instead, he took a walk along the river and let himself freeze in the cold. At one point near the river's edge, he took off the watch he'd received for Christmas and hurled it into the icy water. A fitting punishment, he thought.

When he got home, he stood just outside the living room and stared at the TV light casting shadows around his mother's hair that was tightly curled around pink rollers. She watched the news, oblivious to his presence, sipping decaf coffee and waiting for her husband to return from the search for the missing child. He went upstairs quietly, undressed, and climbed into bed.

Sleep did not come easily. He kept seeing Patricia's face from the flyer and Larry's tear-stained grief at the searches. He knew that he could end all the suffering, but he didn't know how to end his own. His mother's face flashed into his mind. She'd been through so much already. How was this ever going to end?

Connor woke early the next morning. He got out of bed and pulled on his jeans and a sweater. He felt his face that was still bruised from last Thursday. He didn't hate Steve Jones, but he didn't like him and didn't think he deserved so much popularity. He knew if the kids at school knew who Steve really was, he'd lose everything. Connor made his way down the stairs to eat breakfast and stopped like he always did at his brother's Marine photo that hung on the wall. He met his brother's eyes and, ignoring his hunger, turned and went back to his room.

He spent the first half of the day in his room thinking about his life and how much he hated it, and then he remembered Mr. Belner's assignment and took out his spiral notebook and began writing about displacement. He started off slowly describing his family. He wrote extensively about Paul and how he somehow kept the family together like a well-placed rug in a room, and how when Paul was deployed, even his letters and Skype sessions with the family were enough to hold things in place, but then he was killed by friendly fire, and everything came apart. If Paul's death had happened differently, maybe everyone could have moved on. Connor wrote about how he no longer felt he had a place with his family, if he ever had.

He looked at what he wrote and then tore it up. It felt like a girl's diary, and he was suddenly embarrassed. He had wanted a diary, though, one with a lock—a place to unload in all the time, but he didn't know any other guys who kept diaries, so he thought he shouldn't get one. His cousin, Doris, had one, and he enviously watched her scribble away last summer when she had stayed with his family for a month.

He left the house at eight in the morning. It was the day after Christmas. He walked through the snow straight to the Wise Owl Café and banged on the back kitchen door. He banged loudly until the door opened.

Thirty-Three

I SPENT THE MORNING ON THE COUCH STARING OUT THE WINdow at the relentless snow. The rotary phone rang twice, but no one left a message. I wanted to phone Rowena but didn't have anything meaningful to say. I just wanted to hear her voice, but I also was afraid the contact might move me to tears, so I did nothing. Just sat there until the phone rang again, and my own father's voice came into the living room through my grandfather's old answering machine. He sounded sad and mad at the same time. I rose slowly and picked up the phone. The receiver felt heavier than I remember.

"Dad?"

"Casey, I can't believe you didn't tell me," he said. "I had to hear it from a hospital social worker."

"Sorry."

"He's my dad, ya know?"

"I know. I just couldn't believe it, and I did call you but didn't think I should leave such sad news in a voice mail." There was a long pause, and I concentrated on the heat from the steel heating pipes that made creaking sounds all day long.

"Casey?"

"Yeah."

"What do you want to do?"

"What do you mean?"

"I mean do you want to come back to Chicago?"

"No," I said. "I'm fine here. I'm almost done with school, and I have a good job."

"But you're only seventeen," he said. I could tell in his voice that he was relieved. I could feel it. I was relieved too because moving and starting over felt overwhelming. One more semester, and I'd have my diploma. I had Rowena too. I had to stay here in the apartment.

"I'll be eighteen in April, and I'm so close to graduating. I can cook for myself. I'm okay. I can't leave right now."

"Are you sure?"

"Positive."

"Okay. Well, I'm coming down there. We'll put his ashes in the ground."

"Dad?"

"Yeah?"

"I … um … need to scatter his ashes in the river. He wanted that. He told me a long time ago."

"He did?"

"Yeah." My dad didn't say a word for a solid minute. The heater creaked on.

"Okay, but I'm coming down to see you anyway. I'm your dad." We agreed that my dad would come down the day after tomorrow.

I felt restless when I put the receiver down. I wandered around the apartment, straightened up the kitchen, took a load of wash down to the laundry room, and then walked to work. I could have driven the Montego, but visibility wasn't good, and I knew that walking would help get my head cleared out. It always worked in the past.

"Casey, I told you to take a few days off," Andy practically shouted at me.

"I want to work," I said and walked past a couple of staring customers. I hung up my coat and pulled on my rubber apron. Andy followed me back into the heat of the kitchen. His eyes looked weird, antsy and restless. "I don't want to be alone at home right now," I said. His face softened.

"Okay. I get it. But you've been through a lot," he said and put his hands on his hips.

"I know," I said.

"If you decide that you want to leave early, it's okay," he said.

"Thanks."

I did not leave early that night. I worked hard and washed every mug, glass, plate, fork, knife, spoon, ladle, spatula, and pot in the kitchen. I wiped down every table, washed the counters, scrubbed the bathroom, cleaned the mats, swept, mopped. When I hung up my apron, Andy walked over to me and handed me an envelope.

"What's this?"

"It's a post-Christmas bonus. You're the best damn dishwasher I've ever had."

I left the Wise Owl feeling tired but strong. I knew my

grandfather would be proud of me working hard and earning money and not falling over in a ditch bathed in my own tears. Not that he was against crying, but he wouldn't have thought an old man dying was worth crying much over. I smiled thinking about his face laughing and started for home feeling good. My bonus was two hundred dollars, which seemed like a ton of money. I decided that moment to ask Rowena to the movies. My treat. I knew I had to budget the secret tobacco money for rent and groceries, but this was an extra bonus.

I walked through a big snowdrift lost in thought when I saw the light go on in the apartment above the drug store. I had often wondered about Andy's secret affair but never would have dared to ask him about his lady lover. Except it wasn't a lady in the window that drew my attention. It was a child, a little girl with blond hair, and the light went out as quickly as it went on. I stood there staring up at the apartment window hoping the light might flick back on, but it didn't. Of course my mind jumped to the conclusion that the child in the window was Patricia Dale, and I wasn't going to just do nothing, so I set off running to the police station, since Andy had just closed down the café and I couldn't use the phone inside to call 9-1-1. I ran as fast as I could past snowdrifts and stuck drivers cursing the weather. I didn't stop running until I reached the River City Police Station.

"Chief Cole," I said to the uniformed man seated at the information booth. His face was buried behind a newspaper.

"He's out," the man said.

"I think I just saw the missing Dale girl," I said. The man pulled his face out of the newspaper and stood up.

"Just a moment," he said and disappeared into a glassed-off area filled with cubicles. I waited. Another man, this one without a uniform, came out to speak with me.

"What have you seen and where?" I described the scene and then gave him my information. He told me they'd send someone right out. He even said I could ride along so I didn't have to walk back in the cold. I jumped at the chance to ride along.

The patrol car took the main streets to avoid the snow drifts, and we were downtown in five minutes. The drugstore was closed, but the light was on in the apartment upstairs. One officer stepped out of the car, and the other one parked about half a block away. I got out, but the second officer told me to stay by the car. He said something about liability. I moved so I could see. I watched them push buttons on an intercom and wait. The door buzzed, and they disappeared into the building. Several minutes passed, and then they re-emerged and headed towards the car.

"What happened?"

"Nothing. No kid," the driver said.

"But I saw one," I said.

"No kid lives in that unit," the other officer said. "There are no toys. Nothing."

"She could have been moved," I said. The officers looked at each other. I knew they thought this was a dead end, but I knew what I saw.

"You're right. She could have been moved, but we have no way of knowing if that happened. Where do you live, kid? We'll drop ya." As we pulled away from the curb, I stared up at the window and wondered what was going on.

Thirty-Four

CARLY AND STEVE CUDDLED ON STEVE'S NARROW BED WHILE Trevor pretended to play a video game on Steve's PlayStation. He could see Carly and Steve's reflection on the TV screen, and it made him want to scream, so he did. He screamed every time he made a wrong move in the game to mask his growing anger and frustration.

"Dude, keep it down," Steve said.

"I'm losing!"

"So what? Keep it down. My mom likes the house quiet in the evenings."

Trevor turned to face Steve, and Carly smiled at him. Her smile sent a quiver through his body that could not be repressed.

"Carly, I need to tell you something now because if I hold it in any longer I might pull your hair out," Trevor said as calmly as he could.

Carly stared in shock. Steve sat up.

"Steve is my boyfriend even though you think he's yours," he said.

Carly turned to look at Steve.

"Shut up!" he yelled at Trevor.

"But we love each other!"

"Steve," Carly pleaded with big scared eyes.

The yelling from the room brought Martha running down the hall. She tore open the door and flicked on the lights. The kids were staring at each other like street cats preparing to battle.

"What's happening?" Martha asked in a raised voice just below her own yell.

Tears streamed down Trevor's cheeks. He was a dam released.

"Steve's mine. He's mine," he said softly and walked out of the room. Seconds later, he was out the front door.

Carly stared up at her boyfriend, who sunk down onto the bed. Martha waited, confused.

"What did he mean that you love each other?" Carly asked and started to cry.

Steve couldn't meet anyone's eyes. He just stared down at his comforter.

Martha felt worn out. She looked at Steve. "I'll give you two a moment to talk," she said and quietly left the room.

"What's going on? Why did Trevor . . . ?" Carly asked.

"I don't know. He's too attached since his dad and him got into it," Steve said. Carly turned to face Steve. Mascara smears streaked down her cheeks, but she was dry-eyed now.

"I love you, Steve. Do you love me?"

Steve was silent.

Carly stood up and found her coat that had fallen to the floor. She laced up her snow boots and left the room.

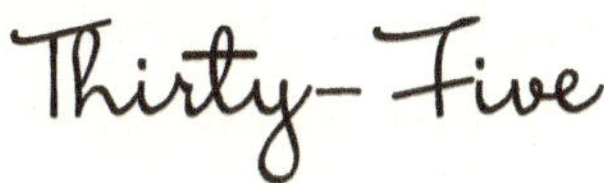

I SAT IN THE BACK OF THE CRUISER AND LISTENED TO THE police radio. The policeman driving occasionally responded to the radio and spoke softly to his partner. My mind couldn't figure out what had happened. I knew what I saw. I was sure of it.

The police cruiser moved gently through the snow while soft shadows from barren trees moved over me as we passed beneath streetlights muted by the falling snowflakes. When they eased down the drive into Sky Court, I thought I saw someone run into the garbage and recycling area. When I stepped out of the car, the policemen told me to keep my eyes and ears open in case I spotted anything worth checking out. I waved goodbye until their headlights disappeared around the corner. I started to head in and then jumped when I felt a hand on my shoulder.

"Hey, it's just me, Trevor," he said shaking. He tried to smile. I stared at Trevor, who stood before me with no coat or gloves. It was freezing.

"What's up?"

"Can I hang at yours for a bit? I'm freezing." I looked at his red cheeks and ears and decided to let him in.

He was grateful for the warmth of the little apartment. He said it looked like the same layout as his and his dad's, but maybe smaller. "How many bedrooms?" he asked.

"Just two," I said and flicked on the light in the kitchen. "Why don't you have a coat on?"

"I walked out of Steve's without thinking," he said and stood awkwardly hugging himself.

I turned the heat up a bit then walked to the closet and pulled out a sweater. It was one of my grandfather's sweaters, and I held on to it for a minute and felt the worn, soft wool.

"Here." I handed him the sweater. "Put this on."

Trevor took it and pulled it on. It was a bit big for him, but he smiled.

"Sit down," I said.

Trevor entered the living room and plopped on the couch. When I switched on the lamp next to the couch I could see that he'd been crying, but he didn't look away. "What's going on, Trevor?"

"My dad found out that I'm gay and wanted to kill me, and I stayed with Steve and his mom, but then Carly showed up just when everything was going great, and she just … she just took all his attention from me, and he's my boyfriend, and, I mean, I love Steve," he said defiantly. So many words were tumbling out of his small mouth. I tried to take it all in. I already knew that Steve and Trevor had a thing, but it did feel strange hearing another kid in high school tell me he was gay. A sound came from the other room. I jumped.

"Shit, I'm sorry," he said. "I probably woke your grandpa."

I rose from the chair and walked slowly down the hall to my grandfather's room. I didn't turn on the light. The blind was up, and the snow's whiteness lit the room. I looked around and spotted his old cane on the floor. He rarely used it, but it must have just fallen. I picked it up and stood there in the silence of his room.

"Where's your grandpa?" Trevor leaned in the doorway behind me.

"He died," I said. "He died on Christmas."

"Oh," Trevor said. "I'm sorry."

I made a pot of coffee, and Trevor and I forged a friendship that night. We talked openly about who we were and how hard it was to be in high school and just be ourselves. I'd never talked about myself so much except with Rowena.

It was just past midnight when Connor's phone rang. I sat bolt upright and ran to the phone. The ringing stopped when I handed it to Trevor.

"This is Connor's from that night in the woods," I said. "I found it after you left. He was filming you."

Trevor took the phone and stared at it. It wasn't locked, so he went to the photos and videos. We watched the video together in silence, then Trevor deleted it. He looked sad. He handed the phone back to me.

"I was gonna give this to you and Steve, but somehow handing it over felt like more than handing over a phone."

"What do you mean?"

"Well, I guess I'd be admitting to knowing about you guys — your relationship," I said, just then realizing that that was how I thought about it. "I guess I wanted to respect your privacy."

Trevor just stared at me.

"What're you gonna do with this phone?" he asked.

"Throw it away, I guess. My grandpa hated cell phones. He wouldn't let me get one. It does keep ringing though." I went to the voice mail section and handed the phone to Trevor. "Do you know how to play the messages?"

Trevor laughed and activated the voice mail. I froze when I heard who the message was from.

"Do you know that voice?"

"Yeah. It's my boss at the café, Andy."

"They know each other?"

"I guess so."

We played the message two times. It wasn't very clear, but Andy sounded mad. The wind messed up part of it, so Andy must have been outside, and he sounded super pissed off about having to move something on his own. I strained to understand what was said. It was pretty garbled. I finally put the phone down.

"Hey, why were you with the cops when I saw you earlier?"

"Oh, I thought I spotted the missing girl — Patricia Dale."

"For real?"

"Yeah, so I ran to the police station, but when we went to check it out, she was gone."

"You're sure you saw her?" Trevor was lying on the living room floor with hands behind his head.

"I'm not positive it was Patricia Dale, but I'm positive I saw a little blond kid. The light was only on for a second."

"I'm too wired to sleep," Trevor said. "Wanna show me where you spotted the missing kid?"

It was nearly two when we left Sky Court. The night was white and cold. I lent Trevor my grandfather's old coat and gloves. The old man's coat looked funny draped over Trevor's slim figure. We walked because I didn't want to risk getting stuck in the snow so late at night. I led Trevor through the woods to Bridge Road to River City's tiny town square. We stopped in front of the now dark Wise Owl Café. The building across the street was the old drugstore. I pointed up at a window.

"That's where I spotted Patricia Dale around nine p.m." Trevor stared and furrowed his brows. "But when I went back with the police, the guy who manages the building said there were no small kids there."

"You sure it was the right apartment? There are a few up there. My brother's girlfriend used to live in that building."

"It was the right place. Someone's messing around. That's all."

"Too much time has passed," Trevor said. "That kid is probably dead."

"What about the recent doll theft?"

"I don't know about that." They walked on past the Wise Owl and back towards Bridge Road. "Casey, would it be okay if I slept at your place? I don't want to face Steve and his mom yet."

"You can sleep on the couch."

Thirty-Six

"CARLY, WAIT!" STEVE LEAPT FROM THE BED AND STOPPED Carly at the door. He took her by the hand and led her to the sofa.

"Mom, can you come here?" he called.

Martha padded softly down the hall in her house shoes and bathrobe. She sat down in the chair across from the sofa and waited patiently. Steve stood before the two women.

"I have been sleeping with Trevor," he said. The words came out calmly, but Steve shook inside. Turbulence filled his stomach, and he swallowed hard.

"So you love him more than me?" Carly looked scared. She held her breath in that question.

Martha waited for his reply.

"I do love you, Carly, but not in the way you want."

Carly began to cry again, big tears. Martha didn't comfort the girl though. She wanted to hear more from her son who had been so closed off and secretive for so long.

"I love Trevor. I don't know if I'm gay. I just really love him."

Martha smiled at Steve, who looked relieved. Carly stopped crying and hugged herself in her coat. Silence filled the apartment.

Steve sat down next to Carly and put his arms around her, but she removed his arms and stared into his eyes.

"Do you hate me?" he asked.

"No," she said. "I wish you would have been honest sooner, but I don't hate you." She stood to leave.

"Goodbye," she said to Martha. Steve walked with her to the door and watched her walk away. He listened to her boots on the concrete until he couldn't hear them any longer, then he sighed.

He felt old when he turned back to his mother. Martha rose from the couch and walked towards her son. She put her arms around him and squeezed tight.

"Thank you for being honest about yourself, Steven. You know I love you no matter what, right?"

"Yeah, Mom. I know."

"We need to find Trevor. There's no way he went back to his father's place. It's cold out there tonight."

They drove through the snow in Steve's newly repaired Ford Focus. Martha had kept Steve in the dark about the insurance negotiations she had struggled through with Larry Dale's employer even though he was clearly at fault. She had laughed when Steve — who didn't know if he'd ever drive that little car again — stepped out into the Sky Court carport on Christmas morning and saw the car looking new with a big red bow stuck on the repaired windshield.

With the high beams on, they had increased visibility, but driving was still rough. Martha looked one way and Steve looked another. They drove around town for forty-five minutes before

Martha spotted a figure on a park bench doubled over. She pulled to the curb and called Trevor's name. When the figure looked up, though, Steve recognized the bloodied face of Connor Cole.

"Connor?" Steve climbed out of the car. Connor rose. He was almost the same height as Steve. His face had been badly beaten. Tiny icicles had frozen to his eyelashes. "Connor, get in the car. We'll take you home." Steve reached out to help him walk to the car.

"Don't touch me, faggot!" Connor ran and then staggered and fell into a snow drift. Steve ran to help him, but he shoved him off and ran away. Steve returned to the car.

"We need to call his father," Martha said.

On the way home, they called Chief Cole, who was thankful for the news. Steve then left his mom on the couch in front of a hot cup of tea and walked to Trevor's apartment, even though he knew he probably wouldn't be there. Dean answered the door after several loud knocks.

"What do you want? It's late," Dean said. Steve could see a half-eaten pizza on the table.

"Is Trevor here?"

"No. Your boyfriend ain't here. I thought he was with you," Dean snarled and then rubbed his stubbly jaw.

Steve turned away without another word. He returned home unsure of what to do next. Before he reached his door, he heard voices coming from the parking lot. He walked toward them and saw Casey and Trevor walking towards the staircase.

"Hey!" he shouted. They turned and saw Steve. Trevor looked sheepish. Steve's eyes weren't mad though. He smiled.

"We've been out looking for you. Me and Mom."

"I've been with Casey," he said. "I'm gonna stay with her tonight."

This announcement surprised Steve, since he was barely friends with Casey himself. He'd never even seen Trevor talk to her. "I wish you'd come home with me," he said.

Trevor's eyes got big.

"We looked everywhere. Thought we found you once, but it was Connor, and he'd had the shit beat out of him," Steve reported.

"Really?" Casey said.

"Yup. He'll have two black eyes for sure. I just hope he doesn't say I did it this time."

"Who beat him up?" Casey asked.

"No idea," Steve said.

Trevor turned to Casey. "Would you mind if I stayed with Steve?"

"Of course not," she said. It was settled. Casey returned to the apartment alone.

Thirty-Seven

CONNOR STAGGERED THROUGH THE SNOW. HE LEANED UP against a telephone pole and tore off the flyer that showed a smiling Patricia Dale. *MISSING*, it read. He tore it up and threw it into the wind. His head hurt. His eye hurt. He was badly cut. But his anger fueled him through his pain. He found a brick near the old flower garden in the city park. He carried it to the front of the Wise Owl and hurled it with all the strength he had left. The crash was loud, and he watched as the big front window splintered into a million glass shards.

"Fuck you!" he shouted. "Fuck you, traitor!" He then ran down the street until he slipped on snow-covered ice and fell hard against a truck, setting off its alarm.

The patrol car rolled up and stopped inches from where his body lay.

"Connor?" Chief Cole lifted his son from the snowbank and walked him to the car. The truck's alarm continued to sound, and the chief drove away without noticing the smashed window at the Wise Owl Café.

Chief Cole didn't speak to his injured son on the slow ride home but dragged him from the cruiser roughly and deposited him into a chair in the bright kitchen of their family home. They sat in front of two cups of coffee. Mrs. Cole stood by the counter pouring her own mug.

"Who did this to you?" Chief Cole, in an old flannel shirt and Dockers didn't look like a cop, just an older man with a crewcut, lines on his face, and sorrowful eyes.

"I don't know," Connor said. "Just some guys leaving Stanley's Bar."

"Stanley's was dead tonight. I cruised by there myself."

"Well, it got lively, and I was walking by, and they jumped me. Some college kids."

"They've all gone home for break."

"Some stay over winter break. You've said so yourself."

"Let's let him rest. He's exhausted," Mrs. Cole said and went to Connor with a bag of frozen peas for his eye.

"No," Chief Cole said. "We get to the bottom of this now."

Chief Cole bore down on his youngest son. Connor felt his father's breath on his damaged face.

"What happened, Connor?" He meant this question in a larger sense, and Connor's eyes filled with tears. His mother rushed to him, but Chief Cole threw up an arm to prevent her hands from reaching her son. She stepped back and pounded the countertop. There was a sound on the back porch, an animal's high-pitched screech, and the chief jumped and pulled open the door. Two large raccoons scurried off the porch. When he turned back to his family, he saw his wife move towards Connor, who stood to his full height and left the room, leaving his wife a heaving, sobbing form. Chief Cole went to his wife and held her. Reluctantly, she surrendered.

Thirty-Eight

I WANTED TO CONTACT LARRY DALE and tell him what I saw, tell him my suspicions, but when I called the contact number on the flyer, all I got was an answering machine. I left my name and number and asked specifically for Larry to return my call. I told him I was the one from the café, the Black dishwasher.

After hanging up, I started cleaning the house in anticipation of my dad's visit. I was kind of excited at the prospect of seeing my dad. I hadn't missed him at all these past few months, but now since he was coming, I felt happy. I started in on cleaning the kitchen, but I stopped at the trash. I could see some old tobacco in the garbage bag and didn't want to throw it out. That would have been my grandfather's last smoke. He must have knocked it out of his pipe just before heading to the hospital. I reached in and touched it. The burnt tobacco just fell apart in my hands. No more than ashes. I wondered if my grandfather looked like this. I was supposed to pick him up in a few days. I decided not to throw out the trash. I'd wait. Maybe my dad would want to see the last of his father's tobacco. It was something.

As I was finishing up the few dishes in the sink, the phone rang. It was my dad.

"Hi, Dad."

"Hi, Case. Look, I need to change our plan a bit," he said.

"What's up?"

"I've got a lot to do here, and I want to come next week instead of today. Things at work just kind of piled up on me all of a sudden. Is that all right with you?"

"Sure," I said.

"Okay. Next week then. We'll go together to pick up my old man's ashes," he said and hung up.

I put the phone down and sat on the couch for a few minutes. I sat there and bawled because I guess I needed to see my dad more than I wanted to admit. The blinds were open, and the snow had finally stopped falling, but the sky was a heavy gray. This was a temporary reprieve.

When I stopped crying, I made a pot of coffee, stayed busy cleaning, and when there was nothing left to clean, I stared out the window at nothing in particular. I re-read my displacement paper and decided not to change anything. "And that's all she wrote," I said when I was done. That's a line my grandpa used to say, so I said it again just to feel better.

I went to Rowena's later in the afternoon to see if she'd go walking with me. Rowena's eyes were tired and her hair was messy. She didn't invite me inside. She stepped outside into the hall and whispered. "My parents got into it last night. Big blowout. My mom's a wreck. I need to stay with her today," she said.

She stepped in close and kissed me lightly on the mouth

and stepped back inside her apartment. I could hear her mother crying. It was a terrible sound.

I felt a bit lost on my own suddenly. I mean, I'm on my own most of the time, but with my dad canceling and Rowena's commitment to prop up her mom, I just felt sad.

I walked the two miles to the river. The streets were very quiet, but when a car did cruise by, the tires made slurping sounds as the snow had become a gray slushy mess.

On my walk, I passed an elderly couple scraping the stairs that lead to their front door. They waved and looked exhausted. I waved back. A Siamese cat peered from their front window. It looked warm and satisfied watching its owners work so hard.

The crematorium was a separate brick building that was part of the larger River City Funeral Home complex. I waved at the building. I knew my grandfather couldn't wave back, but he was in there resting in an urn or a plastic bag waiting for me to collect his remains after all the paperwork cleared. The big river ran behind the complex of buildings and grounds, and though parts were frozen solid, there was still some bird life cruising above the water. Crows especially seem to love winter. It was a mostly quiet, peaceful scene. The whole day felt frozen except for that moment at the river. I cried there alone on the shore where the river water was free to crash against the sheet piling. I cried because I always seemed to be alone with heavy stuff, and sometimes I did need somebody. I'm not as tough as I seem.

As I watched the river, I began to daydream about being a tugboat captain, piloting a tractor tug, maneuvering two 3,000 horsepower engines, and harnessing all that power to tow or push freighters to dock. The image of me at the helm, ramming through six inches of ice to guide a stuck vessel to safety or open up a shipping lane made me smile. I didn't know all the steps to my goal, but I'd researched getting a job as a deckhand and knew I needed to graduate from high school. I knew I might have to attend a maritime school. The thought comforted me. I really did have a future.

Thirty-Nine

LARRY DALE HAD LOST WEIGHT IN THE LAST FEW WEEKS FROM missed meals. He had lost his job at the truck company in Galesburg, and he spent every waking minute of every day searching for his daughter. Since Patricia's disappearance, his suspended license had been overlooked by the police, and he drove his own battered '67 Ford truck through the snow and ice of River City often without going to sleep. He walked through forgotten culverts and fallow fields. He staggered through alleyways and wandered through private yards. He didn't care. He was determined to get his child back.

A few days after Christmas, he staggered into the Wise Owl and ordered a bowl of soup and some crackers. Larry buried his face in the bowl and devoured the split pea soup like he had forgotten how good food could taste. Andy stood back and offered him coffee. Larry accepted and then took a breather from eating. His bloodshot eyes finally focused on Andy.

"Andy?"

"Yeah," Andy said. He poured the coffee and then shoved a cream container to Larry.

"I need to say something to you," he said. He pushed his soup bowl aside and focused on Andy's face.

"What?"

"Hey, man, I'm really sorry about what happened between us in high school," Larry said and rubbed his thinning hair. He looked hard at Andy, and their eyes met. Andy turned away and straightened up the silverware behind him. "Andy, I mean it, man. I was such a jerk to so many people. I'm sorry I hurt you. I wasn't as strong as you!"

Andy turned to look at Larry, who had been so tall and strong once. Now, Larry Dale was a crumpled, overweight, terrified father. Andy walked into the kitchen. "Andy!" Larry called out in a strained voice. Customers stared at him, and he sat back down on his stool.

I entered work through the kitchen door because my boots were wet and dirty with snow caked into the sole. I saw Andy standing by his little desk. I took off my coat and hat and hung it up before I walked over to him.

"Andy?"

He whipped around and shouted, "What?"

I stepped back shaken.

"Oh, Casey, I'm sorry. I'm on edge. I thought you were some-one else."

"You pissed about the smashed window?"

"Yeah, yeah. I just … I'm on edge today. Lack of sleep. The window's gonna be fixed soon. High school kids probably," he said and tried to laugh. I didn't buy it. I stepped away from my boss and put on my apron. I was too tired to try and figure out what adults were thinking or feeling. My own insides were enough. I went to work. When I took a break at the counter, I was surprised to see Larry Dale on a stool asleep.

Andy set a fresh cider donut down in front of me and smiled. I smiled back at him but could see in his eyes something was off. He looked tormented. His eyes were not really focused on me or the donut. Then I saw the bruises. His knuckles were dried blood and scabby.

"What happened to your hand?"

"Oh, I hurt it, um, trying to get out of a ditch. Got stuck," he said and backed away into the kitchen. I remembered Steve's report about Connor's beaten face and then I remembered Connor coming here to the back kitchen door. It was Andy's voice on Connor's phone.

Larry snored, and I shook him awake. It took several seconds for him to blink into consciousness and recognize the person shaking him.

"Larry?"

"Hey. Hi, you," he said.

"Larry," I said and checked to see if Andy was still in the kitchen. "Larry, I saw Patricia last night."

"What?" Larry sat up straight and grabbed me by the apron.

"I saw her across the street in an apartment on the second floor." Larry jumped off the stool and ran out the front door. He ran across the street and was almost hit by a car. I chased after him. The wind whipped around us, and the cold bit into my bare arms. We stopped in the doorway to the drugstore in front of a row of apartment intercom buttons.

"Larry, wait! I told the police. They checked. No one was there. The lady at the apartment said there was never a kid there. But I saw a blond kid in that window." I pointed up. Larry breathed heavily and began banging on all the intercom buttons. Finally, an older man in coveralls opened the entrance door. I rubbed my arms covered in goose bumps.

"Whaddaya want?" the building manager asked.

"The apartment upstairs, second on the right," Larry nearly screamed. "That the one?" He looked at me with his wild eyes.

"This again. Hey, kid, you was here with the cops last night. I told them nobody was here matching the description. The Lassiters are sick of being bothered."

"Lassiters?" I asked and turned to Larry. "Your ex-wife's parents?"

"Yeah, Tom Lassiter owns this building," the older man said. "I'm the building manager."

Larry looked at me. I tried to understand the connection. The missing child, Andy's knuckles, Connor's beaten face, the Lassiters, the phone messages.

Forty

Dean Morrison opened the door quickly. It was late, and his back ached. He wanted to lie down with his heating pad—the only comfort he had left in life. Jay stood before him with his big duffel bag. Dean stepped aside so his older son could enter.

"Why are you back?"

"Diane asked me to leave," Jay said. He moved some beer cans so he could sit down on the couch.

"She got sick of you?"

"She been acting weird the last few weeks. Won't say where she's going, sneaking out to answer the phone. I don't know. We were never solid, I guess. She's way too old for me anyway."

Dean laughed hard at that and sat down in his chair. He yawned and looked at Jay, who reminded him so much of his dead wife, Linda. "Maybe she got another guy?" Jay just shrugged and looked around the apartment.

"Where's Trev?" Jay asked.

"He's with his boyfriend."

"He might as well just move in with Steve. He's always there," Jay said.

"He pretty much has," Dean said.

"Why?"

"I blew up at him and scared him out of the house. He's a fag now, and Steve probably is too."

"What're you talking about? They've always been friends."

"They're a couple of homos. I'm almost one hundred percent sure of that. And Steve's mom, Martha, is just gonna let him do his thing, and she's a sensible woman, so I'm lost." Dean scratched his crotch and sat back. Jay watched him stare at the ceiling. There was a soft knock on the door, and then the door opened. It was Trevor. He entered slowly but smiled when he saw Jay.

"What're you doing here?" Trevor asked.

"Got kicked out. Diane's as bad as her older sister, Katrina. She is one moody little person." Trevor watched his father for signs of violence, but Dean remained seated, staring up at the ceiling. "Dad says you're gay now. Is that true?"

"Yeah," Trevor said.

Dean turned to face his son then. His eyes were not hard, but he was silent.

"I just came to get more underwear and clothes."

"Grab my heating pad while you're down there, weirdo," Dean said.

Trevor walked down the hall to collect his things. He looked at his old room and went to the dresser. Slowly he went through his clothes deciding what to take and what to leave. His baseball mitt was nicely worn in. It had been a gift from his dad several years ago, and though he didn't love baseball, he loved that his dad had given him such a special glove. He'd take it with him. He sat on his bed and looked at the room as if he was never coming back. He felt like crying, but then Jay hovered into view.

"Hey, Trev," he said from the doorway.

"Hey," Trevor said back.

"So are you and Steve really together? Like boyfriends?"

Trevor looked at his older brother. Jay looked tired, and his jeans were dirty. His flannel shirt looked slept in.

"I love Steve," he said.

"Wow. I did not see this coming," Jay said. He walked all the way into the room and plopped on the bed. Trevor grabbed a shirt from his closet and another pair of jeans. "How long have you known you were gay?"

"A long time, bro."

"You never said anything."

"'Cause this is, like, the most understanding household."

"Good point," Jay said, and they both laughed. "Maybe if Mom was around you would have said something."

"Maybe." Trevor shrugged and then zipped up his torn, nylon bag. Trevor watched Jay get off the bed and walk up to him. Jay surprised him with a tight hug.

"Love you, man," Jay said.

"Love you too."

Trevor walked to the front door as Dean opened another can of beer and sipped it. He tossed the heating pad to his dad, and Dean caught it with one big hand.

"Hey, mister," he said to Trevor.

"What?"

"Don't be a stranger," he mumbled and then sucked down the rest of the beer.

Trevor closed the door quietly and walked back to Steve's apartment.

Forty-One

"MY MOM WANTS TO MEET YOU. SHE HAS A THING ABOUT WANT-ing to know who I'm hanging out with. Are you up for that?" Rowena surprised me with a visit. The evening had been painfully lonely, so I was happy to see her face.

"Sure," I said. She wrapped her arms around me and put her head on my shoulder.

"I think you're starting to smell like your grandfather," she said. "Like a sweet tobacco that I could easily become addicted to." I laughed, and she squeezed me harder. I took Rowena's hand and walked her to my bedroom.

"I haven't slept here since he died," I said. We stood staring into each other's eyes in the doorway. In that moment, I felt a warmth surge through my whole body, and the only name I could think to call it was love. Rowena kissed me gently on the lips, and then the cell phone that I meant to destroy rang. I picked it off the bookshelf and stared at the number. This time it was different. A name came up: Dad. Connor must not have told his dad that he lost his phone. No message was left. I set the phone down, and Rowena took my hand and led me to my twin bed. Clothes came off slowly.

It was after one o'clock in the morning when I heard knocking. I pulled on a t-shirt and sweatpants and walked to the door.

"I'm Barbara Miller, Rowena's mother. Is she here?" A shorter and older version of Rowena stood before me.

"Come in. I'm Casey, Mrs. Miller." We shook hands, and I noticed her hand was soft and warm, even though her face was hard. "I'll go get Rowena." I woke her gently with light kisses on the neck. I didn't realize that her mom had followed me down the hall and watched as we embraced. Rowena stopped when she saw her mother's look of surprise.

"Sorry, Mom. I should have told you I was going to sleep over. I wasn't sure. It just happened." Mrs. Miller remained silent and waited for Rowena, who unabashedly embraced me again and kissed me on the lips. I felt shy with a witness. I said goodbye quietly and then walked them both to the front door.

When Rowena left, I was overcome with sadness. She'd only been gone for an hour, and I missed her so much. Maybe I'm not the lone ranger I'd always thought I was.

I sat on the couch and thought about the events of the past few weeks. I hoped that Trevor was okay. My mind kept going back to the kid in the window, to Larry Dale's face, to that damn cell phone with the ability to videotape private moments, to Steve saying that Connor was beat up, and Andy's bruised knuckles, and the café's smashed front window. I sat there for an hour rolling all these faces and ideas around in my head, trying to see a connection. Was it possible that my boss was somehow connected to the disappearance of Patricia Dale? I mean that was crazy thinking, but his busted up knuckles didn't make sense. Stuck car? I didn't buy it. I've always trusted Andy, but something didn't add up.

I got up, made coffee, and then sat back down. I remembered Andy showing me his scar and how mad it made him, how pissed off at Larry he was for some teenage cruelty dealt out years ago. But was he still mad about it? Mad enough to kidnap Larry's kid? Could my boss be a criminal? I found it hard to accept. Andy could be moody, but he was also funny and gave me a holiday bonus — but I never shoved him down any stairs.

For no good reason other than sleeplessness, I got dressed and pulled on my boots and coat. I set out into the snow. I walked to the Wise Owl. Was this women's intuition? I don't know, but I like to go with my gut, and when I arrived, I could see light seeping out around the edges of the wooden boards that had been used to cover the gaping hole in the front window frame. I could also see that Andy's car was parked in the lot next door. Maybe he was crunching numbers. Maybe the café was in trouble, and that's why he seemed anxious and extra moody. Maybe he stole some man's child and hid her for unknown reasons.

I stood across the street and waited. The street was dark except for a streetlight that was on at the end of the block. Christmas was over, and I had to return to school in one week, but returning to my old routine wouldn't change the fact that my life had changed dramatically. I had to be extra responsible now because I was on my own.

I was thinking about my grandfather's face and smile when the snow began to fall. It started out light, the way snow often does, but it picked up pretty fast. Then the kitchen door at the side of the building opened and Andy came outside. He pulled up the collar on his coat and got into his late model Subaru Legacy. If I had driven the Montego, I could stick to him, but as there was no traffic, and plenty of snow, I followed his tire tracks on foot. I slogged through the increasing snowfall, following my instincts when I lost sight of the tracks.

I ended up at the Super 8 Motel near the River City hospital. It was one of only two motels in town. The other one is attached to the college and kind of pricey according to the kids at school. I spotted his car parked in the motel lot. I studied the motel looking for signs of life at this late hour. There was only one light on at the motel, room number four. The curtain was drawn, so I couldn't see into the room at all, but now I had something to tell the police. Room number four. Something told me they might find a child in that room.

I walked quickly back to Sky Court so that I could call the cops. When I got home, my dad was standing outside the door to the apartment rubbing his hands and pacing in a tight circle. When he saw me, he smiled.

CONNOR SNUCK BACK INTO HIS HOME AT THREE IN THE morning. He climbed through the basement window that he had propped open earlier and walked back up to his bedroom.

Chief Cole was waiting for him.

"Where have you been, son?"

Connor said nothing. Chief Cole took another good look at his son's beat up face.

"Son, who did this to you?"

Connor looked at his dad's stark face that had creases on the cheeks but still said nothing.

Chief Cole reached out to touch Connor, but the boy recoiled as if a snake had tried to bite him. His moment of sympathy passed like a bolt through a cattle prod, and he grabbed his son by the coat and shoved him to the wall.

"What's wrong with you, boy?"

Connor stayed silent as his dad delivered a hard slap.

"Answer me!"

He received another hard slap to the jawline. His eyes watered. He wanted to crumble to the floor and cry out for his mother, but he didn't. He took another slap, and then Chief Cole stopped.

He wasn't looking at his son anymore. He was staring at his bed, where the arm of a doll was dangling from beneath the mattress. He strode the length of the small room and ripped the baby doll from beneath the twin mattress. He held the doll out in front of him as if he were examining a suspect. When he turned to question Connor, the boy ran from the room and nearly tumbled down the stairs.

Forty-Three

I WAS SURPRISED TO SEE MY DAD. I HADN'T EXPECTED HIM UN-
til next week, but there he was. He'd grown a beard, which was
strange. We hugged, and after I unlocked the front door, I went
straight to the phone to call the police.

"What's going on?"

"I'll be right with you," I said.

Chief Cole wasn't in. It was too early. I wanted to speak to
him, not one of the patrol cops who didn't believe that I'd seen
Patricia in the apartment above the pharmacy. I decided to call
back later. I put the coffee pot on and rubbed my hands together.
I was still freezing cold.

I then called Larry Dale's contact number on the flyer, but I
reached an answering machine. I realized it was four thirty in the
morning and put the phone down. This would all have to wait.

"Aren't you glad to see me?"

"Yeah, of course, Dad," I said. It was hard to concentrate on
his face because he kept smiling, even though his hands were
fidgety and he seemed stressed. I noticed he had more forehead
lines than I'd ever seen before.

"I know I'm early, but I decided to leave and just come here because you probably needed me."

I didn't know what to say to that. I loved my dad and even missed him, but I hadn't needed him for a long time. He sent me down here when I was barely fifteen, and he rarely visited. He called a lot at first, and we had a good phone relationship, but he chose his new wife over me. I got grandpa, and he got a new family, and that's how it was. Those were the facts. And now Grandpa was dead. His body was just ashes now, his spirit floating around awaiting its next assignment. His sweet-smelling pipe smell still lived in the apartment, but Ernest Black was dead. I accepted that. I knew I wasn't getting anymore surprise dinners from the chicken farm.

"Dad, here's some coffee," I said and handed him a mug.

"Thank you," he said and sipped. He looked around the apartment and then at me.

"So how you doing, kid?" My dad tried on another smile, but his face was pretty broken. His eyebrows roved all over his forehead. I couldn't ignore it.

"Dad, I'm okay. You look pretty stressed though."

He set his coffee down and sat back. I watched him. He sighed hard. His beard had gray strands in it. He looked kind of chunky too. Something was off.

"Mirlayna and I are having some struggles. Grown-up stuff," he said and tried that weak smile on again.

"So are you guys still living together?"

He hesitated, and I could tell by his rumpled clothes and scraggly beard that he was probably on his own like me, except I took better care of myself.

"Well, yes, I mean, I'm probably gonna have to find my own place eventually. We're trying to work out a way to both get our needs met, and I —"

Connor's phone rang, and I jumped to my feet. I ran down the hall. I answered it because it was his dad.

"Chief Cole?"

"Yes. Who is this?"

"Casey Black, from the search party. Room four at the Super 8 Motel. I think Patricia Dale is in there!"

"Wait, slow down. Who is this? Why do you have my son's phone?"

"I found it in the woods and meant to return it. Room four at the Super 8 Motel," I said again. By this time my dad had walked down the hallway and stared at me.

"Did you steal my son's phone?"

"Chief Cole, I can't explain everything right now. It's kind of an emergency. Please just go to the Super 8 Motel, room four. I have a hunch the missing girl is there."

"Casey, what's going on?" My dad stood in the doorway frowning at me through his new beard.

"I'm looking for my son," Chief Cole said. "Do you know where he is?"

"No! You need to get to the Super 8 Motel. I'm telling you, Patricia Dale has got to be there."

I didn't have time for any of this. I hung up the phone, ran past my dad, grabbed the car keys and my coat.

"Be back soon," I said.

The early morning air bit into my face, but I drove fast through slick streets with the windows down because the snow was coming down hard and visibility was poor. I skidded into the Super 8 parking lot and put the car into park. I kept it running with the heater on. No room lights were on. Too early I guess.

I went to room four and knocked. What did I have to lose? I knocked hard again.

To my surprise, the door opened to reveal Connor's bruised and swollen face. He didn't even look surprised to see me. He just stood there.

I pushed passed him and entered the room. He didn't try to stop me.

The room was a typical motel room with two double beds, a table, a chair, and a TV on a console. The TV was on, but the volume was muted, so I just saw the faces of the morning news people moving their mouths. The bathroom door was open, and a faint light drifted from within. It illuminated a pile of stuffed animals in a corner. There was food from the Wise Owl on the table. I recognized the containers. Connor closed the door and sat down on the bed nearest it. A small figure slept soundly in the other bed.

"Is that Patricia Dale?" I whispered.

"Yeah," he said.

"Are you in on this with Andy?"

"Yeah."

"What happened to your face?"

"Andy was mad about me losing the phone and not telling him for so long, then my loving father added a few smacks," he said. Connor's head hung low. It was strange seeing him so defeated.

I wanted to know exactly why my boss had gotten involved with this scheme, but I figured it would all come out later. Without saying another word, I gently lifted Patricia Dale off the bed, keeping a blanket wrapped around her. Connor just watched.

Patricia barely stirred. She was light as a cat. I walked her toward the door, and Connor rose. He stood in front of the door for a long moment with his back to me and his hand on the doorknob.

"I'm really not a bad person," he whispered. "Things just got out of hand." He opened the door, and I stepped out of room number four. "I just didn't know how to end it," was the last thing I heard him say.

Chief Cole's police cruiser pulled into the parking lot. He had listened to me after all. A moment later, my dad pulled in and parked in front of the Montego. I walked slowly towards the men with the sleeping child in my arms. Chief Cole walked towards me. I handed Patricia Dale to him.

"She's asleep. Connor's inside," I said.

Chief Cole frowned, turned back to his cruiser, and placed the bundled child inside. He approached me slowly. The snow came down hard now, but I could see his face. "How'd you know about all this?"

"I saw my boss's bruised knuckles, and my neighbor told me he saw Connor's beaten face. I followed my boss to this place earlier, and it all added up." Chief Cole was silent as the snow covered his crewcut. He looked so tired.

My dad came over to me and just stared. That's when we heard the shot. We all jumped. There was a moment between the blast and the sound of Chief Cole's boots rushing through the sludge. He ran to the room and threw open the door.

"Connor!" he shouted.

Part Three

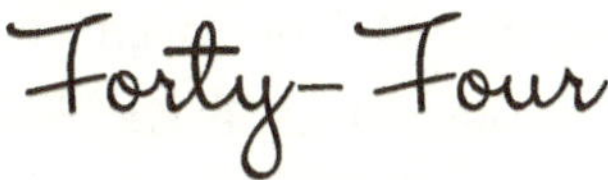

THE PHONE RANG AT SEVEN IN THE MORNING ON MY BIRTHDAY. It was April. Chilly and sunny. A perfect day for an eighteenth birthday.

"Happy birthday," my dad said. I pictured his grayish beard and his tired eyes.

"Thanks, Dad," I said.

"What are you gonna do for your birthday?"

"Go to work," I said.

The spring semester began at River City High with more than three feet of snow on the ground. If the school had resided within a large city, classes would surely have been canceled. Rowena was no longer in English class with me. She stayed home and sat in front of a computer because, at the last minute, the school board unanimously voted to add an online program. She sat in the living room for three hours each day and worked independently. Occasionally she needed to visit the library or do some field research, but for the most part, she had successfully avoided returning to school. She saw me some evenings. Our time always felt special because I knew there was an expiration date in the near future. I missed seeing her face in school, but I understood her need for independence. In March, Rowena received an early acceptance letter from Middlebury College. I was happy for her because I knew that's what she wanted, but I felt sad for me because the only woman I ever loved was gonna go far away, and we would not be living happily ever after. I knew Rowena had visions of living abroad and smoking her foreign cigarettes and being a global citizen. I admired that, but I wanted to work on the river in the Midwest and cut through ice and pull freighters to the shore, and be my own person.

Trevor, Steve, and I formed an unlikely alliance at school and began eating lunch together at the small table near the window where I used to sit at alone. Trevor and Steve were accepted to the same community college with full basketball scholarships. Steve turned down his scholarship to the University of Illinois. By the time the snow had melted, they were both free of their casts as well as several friends who were bothered by their change of lunchroom seating. They did not openly embrace each other at school, but the kids knew. Carly stopped by the new smaller table though. Her love for Steve seemed to remain intact, but not in a romantic way. She offered warm hugs and a big smile and even made an effort to get to know me.

Chief Cole resigned as River City Chief of Police, and another senior officer led the kidnapping investigation, which included inspecting the chief's dead son's cell phone and long interviews with Andy Hardwick and Diane Lassiter, Patricia's aunt, who forever lived in her big sister Katrina's shadow. The *River City Current* reported the convoluted soap opera-like tale of Andy Hardwick's ancient but well-maintained anger with Larry Dale and manipulation of Larry's sister-in-law, Diane. Andy even convinced a lost and lonely Connor Cole to join him in his quest for revenge. After reading the story, I still had questions. A kidnapping just didn't add up. I'd worked for Andy for nearly three years and knew him a little bit. I also knew that a newspaper article was just that — a news story. It wasn't necessarily the whole truth. I wasn't satisfied with the ending.

Connor could no longer speak for himself, but Andy told police that Connor wanted to strike out at his father, who he said never loved him and couldn't see past the memory of his older brother, Paul. Andy, Diane, and Connor worked together to get back at people who wounded them in the past.

The whole town seemed shrouded in the gray of winter until the middle of March, when the birds began to sing again, plum trees blossomed, and the bright sun melted the remaining snow. After the judge heard the testimony from all the parties involved, she sat with Larry Dale for some time in her chambers in the courthouse in the middle of the town square. Only a reporter and a photographer from the *Current* were waiting outside the judge's chamber. The rest of the town seemed to have moved on and buried the whole sad story along with Connor. Surprisingly, Larry did not want to press charges. He and Katrina agreed to share joint custody of Patricia. In the paper, Larry is quoted as saying, "I'm very happy to have my best friend back." Next to the article is a photo of a smiling father and daughter.

Even though school was almost over, and I'd received A's on all my papers, including my character sketch on Larry and my displacement paper about myself, I had the opportunity to do an extra credit paper on unresolved feelings. Mr. Belner had delivered this assignment to a bunch of confused-looking teenagers, myself included. Unresolved feelings? As soon as he started talking about it, I felt way too young to write a paper about this topic. It felt like a paper I could write when I was maybe forty, definitely not now. But I knew someone I could interview: Andy.

Even though Larry Dale told the judge he didn't want to press charges, kidnapping in the State of Illinois is a class two felony. Andy received a sentence of three years of probation. I had spotted him recently cleaning leaves from gutters at his parent's house, so I decided to stop by after school and ask to interview him. He said yes and invited me into his apartment that was above the garage. The tiny space was airy and bright, and Andy seemed almost like his old self. He made us coffee and told me he missed seeing me. It was awkward, but I was happy to see him too.

Andy's face seemed lighter than I'd thought it would. As we settled in to talk, he looked past me, to the big window behind me. The sky was blue and clear. His eyes looked pure and open. His hair was grayer than ever.

"Why did you take Patricia Dale, Andy?" That was my opening question. It was the only one I needed. Andy looked straight at me. His shoulders relaxed, and he sighed. He seemed eager to share his story.

"I didn't set out to hurt anybody, Casey. This goes way back. I mean this was high school stuff that I never resolved." There was that word. I sipped my coffee and waited for more. He sipped his coffee and bit his lower lip. "When I was in high school, I fell in love with someone who I thought loved me back. We met detasseling corn. It was one of those summer nights that are so humid and hot. God. We left the farm and drove out to that old quarry near the old junk yard."

"The Black Cat Junk Yard? I know it."

"Yeah, well, we swam in that quarry until our bodies were cleaned off, and we could put the day behind us, and then when we started to get dressed, he grabbed me, and I thought we were wrestling, but it became sexual, and you know how strong he is." I knew he meant Larry Dale. I didn't say his name, but just nodded my head. "Well, that night started it. We went back to the quarry every night until the end of summer. But when school started up, he ignored me. I lost my head. I attacked him one day, and he threw me down the stairs. That's why I have that scar.

"I had a void for so many years, Casey. I dated women and men and never got that love feeling back that I had for him. Thirty years passed. I saw him with Patricia in the grocery store in August, I think. She was so happy. He was making faces—really making her laugh, and I just felt this stabbing in my heart. I thought I had moved on and put all that pain behind me, but I didn't. I guess I thought that stealing his kid would punish him somehow and make me less miserable. I was a selfish idiot. There wasn't even much of a plan. I recruited Connor 'cause I knew he hated his dad and wanted to give him a crime he couldn't figure out. I got Diane Lassiter involved because we needed a babysitter. It only took a few dates to hook her. She was always jealous of beautiful

Katrina, and I knew she had a soft spot for me. I was a total asshole user, Casey. It was so easy to manipulate those two for my own purposes. Poor Patricia. I took some vulnerable people, especially Connor, to a very dark place. That's what I feel really bad about."

My coffee was cold when Andy finished his story. We shook hands when I left. Walking back to Sky Court I thought about Andy's unresolved feelings, and I decided not to go for the extra credit. It all felt too personal to put down on paper and hand in for a school assignment. It was raw, human suffering that ended in a death.

Even though River City is a small town, I never saw Andy again after our talk. I think he may have hidden himself away. The Wise Owl, with its boarded up front window and sad Christmas tree leaning against the cash register, never re-opened.

With graduation nearing, our time together is precious, so Rowena walks me to my new job most days. We hold hands and walk slower and slower as we approach the little restaurant with the golden lotus statue by the front door because we want to savor the moment. When we stop just a few feet from the door, our eyes meet, we smile at each other, and Rowena always says, "I miss you already," then we kiss. My new boss, Mr. Chu, nods to me and I head straight to the kitchen, put on my rubber apron, and start in on a big stack of dishes. The sounds of the kitchen envelope me, and I smile as I load detergent into the dishwasher.

Acknowledgments

The publication of *Sky Court* was made possible by a talented group of people. Without their help, only my roommate would have read this story. First, I was blessed with the multi-talents of Vinnie Kinsella. He was not only a skillful and compassionate editor but also an amazing book designer.

Big thanks go to Jessie Glenn, Emily Keough, Ivory Fields, and the whole team at Mindbuck Media for tirelessly promoting the book and sharing it with the world.

Finally, I have to thank my best friend and first reader, Deidre J. Williams, for her encouragement, good humor, and diplomatic feedback.

Share Your Opinion

Did you enjoy *Sky Court*? Then please consider leaving a review on Goodreads, your personal blog, or wherever readers can be found. At Circuit Breaker Books, we value your opinion and appreciate when you share our books with others.

Visit circuitbreakerbooks.com for news and giveaways.

FAITH MOSLEY has been telling stories since her childhood, when she and her brother would type up their tales on their beloved orange Olivetti typewriter and then carefully bind them together into books. Over the years, she has worked as a dishwasher, a shipping clerk, an AmeriCorps recruiter, a teacher, a financial aid officer, a claims assistant for the VA, a career development specialist, and a GED intake specialist. She earned a master's degree in journalism from the University of Iowa and a bachelor's in liberal arts from Western Illinois University. Her work was included in the anthology *Lez Talk: A Collection of Black Lesbian Short Fiction* (BLF Press, 2016). She now lives in Central New Mexico, where she has spent the past couple of years converting a small school bus into a tiny house on wheels. *Sky Court* is her first novel.

www.ingramcontent.com/pod-product-compliance
Lightning Source LLC
Chambersburg PA
CBHW030625190726
48286CBV00008B/2395

9781953639141